'Were you ever going to let me know?' Jamie asked.

'Let you know what, exactly?'

'That I had fathered a child?'

'Are you so sure that it's yours?' Sarah bit back, and then immediately regretted the words. Of course he had to know it was his. Despite the fact he had made it clear that he'd never wanted children, he did have the right to know. Even if he wanted nothing to do with either of them.

'Not mine?' For a moment hope flared in his deep brown eyes. Sarah felt as if her heart had been squeezed.

Jamie strode towards her, his mouth set in a grim line. Involuntarily, Sarah stepped back, hugging Calum protectively. Jamie shot her a look of questioning anguish before gently moving aside the blanket covering the small body. The baby gazed up at him with solemn brown eyes. A tiny hand reached out and wrapped itself around one of Jamie's fingers. The child pulled the finger into his mouth. Jamie's heart lurched.

TOP-NOTCH DOCS

He's not just the boss, he's the best there is!

These heroes aren't just doctors,
they're life-savers.

These heroes aren't just surgeons,
they're skilled masters. Their talent and
reputation are admired by all.

These heroes are devoted to their patients.
They'll hold the littlest babies in their arms,
and melt the hearts of all who see.

These heroes aren't just medical professionals.
They're the men of your dreams.

He's not just the boss, he's the best there is

DR CAMPBELL'S SECRET SON

BY
ANNE FRASER

MILLS & BOON®
Pure reading pleasure

First published in Great Britain 2007
Large Print edition 2008
Harlequin Mills & Boon Limited,
Eton House, 18-24 Paradise Road,
Richmond, Surrey TW9 1SR

ISBN: 978 0 263 19949 9

Set in Times Roman 17 on 20 pt.
17-0408-53344

Printed and bound in Great Britain
by Antony Rowe Ltd, Chippenham, Wiltshire

Anne Fraser was born in Scotland, but brought up in South Africa. After she left school she returned to the birthplace of her parents, the remote Western Islands of Scotland. She left there to train as a nurse before going on to university to study English Literature. After the birth of her first child, she and her doctor husband travelled the world, working in rural Africa, Australia and Northern Canada. DR CAMPBELL'S SECRET SON is her first novel, and the hospital which has such a strong hold on Jamie's loyalty is based on the place Anne and her husband lived and worked for a year and a half. It is also the setting for her next book. Anne still works in the health sector. To relax, she enjoys spending time with her family, reading, walking and travelling.

This is Anne Fraser's
debut Medical™ Romance!

To my sisters—
without whom this book
may never have been written!

CHAPTER ONE

SARAH JANE CARRUTHERS took a deep breath before pushing open the double doors and entering the accident and emergency department.

'You'll be OK, girl,' she told herself. After all, it was what she had been working for as long as she could remember. It was the culmination of years of hard work and personal sacrifice. And nobody, except perhaps her mother, knew just how much it had cost her to be here today. One of the youngest and most highly regarded accident and emergency consultants in the country.

Her mind flew back to her mother and baby. It was the first time she had left Calum for a whole day since he had been born six months ago. Although she had tried to prepare them both for this day, she had been surprised at how emotional she had felt leaving her baby. She had been close to tears as she'd handed the small bundle over to her mother.

'We'll be fine, Sarah Jane,' her mother had attempted to comfort her. 'I've got the milk in the fridge and, remember, I have done this once or twice before!' She was the only person who ever called her by her full given name. Sarah preferred to leave out the 'Jane', especially professionally. It made her sound too young.

'I know Mum. It's just that he's so small still. He needs me so much. Maybe I should have stayed off another couple of months. Just until he was a little bigger.'

'It's never going to get any easier, darling. Your work needs you, too. Oh, by the way, did I tell you? You look fantastic.'

Having spent the last few months in jeans and T-shirts, Sarah had taken a great deal of time over her appearance that morning, dressing carefully in a smartly tailored black suit that emphasised her slim figure. She had added a blouse of emerald green which perfectly matched her eyes and tied her thick blonde hair into a neat chignon at the nape of her neck.

Although she had the utmost confidence in her medical ability, this was the first time, as a new consultant, that the buck would stop with her. Her team would be looking to her to take the lead and to inspire confidence. At the very least, she thought with some satisfaction when she had checked her appearance in the mirror, she would look the part, even if she didn't feel it.

However, the moment she stepped into the department it was as if she had never been away. The rush of adrenaline she had always felt coursed through her body, reminding her that despite her love for Calum she also loved being a doctor. And she knew she was a damn good one.

A red-haired nurse, who she recognised from her previous visit to the department, came rushing up to her.

'Dr Carruthers. Welcome to the department. It's good to have you on board. I'm not sure you remember from your visit, but I'm Sister Elizabeth York. My friends call me Lizzie.'

Lizzie's bright smile was infectious and as

Sarah smiled back she felt herself relax. 'It's good to be here,' she replied, surprised to find herself really meaning it.

'Dr MacDonald will be so sorry he can't be here to help you settle in, but the locum who is covering for him is excellent.'

Sarah felt a small flicker of anxiety. Dr MacDonald was the senior consultant and Sarah had relied on him being there. Unfortunately he'd had a small stroke a couple of weeks before and was unlikely to be returning to work. There was nothing for it—she would just have to cope.

'No problem. I'm sure we'll manage. Perhaps you could show me around and introduce me to everyone?'

'Of course, I'd love to. Er, just one thing before we get started,' Lizzie said with a broad grin. 'You have something suspect on the shoulder of your jacket.'

Sarah glanced down. She was aghast to find that Calum had left a little of his breakfast on her shoulder. So far her day wasn't starting exactly as planned! 'Oops. Must have happened when I gave my son a last cuddle on the way out.'

'It's a relief to know you're not perfect after all. We've heard so much about the wonderful Dr Carruthers I was beginning to believe you couldn't be human. One of those wonder-women, juggling a high-flying career and family while managing to look completely gorgeous and immaculate at the same time!'

Sarah laughed. She suspected that she had found a friend and ally in Lizzie. 'Oh, I'm human all right—as you're sure to find out. Give me a few minutes to clean up and then perhaps you can introduce me to the rest of the staff. And thanks. Wasn't exactly the first impression I was hoping to create. I was going with the high-flying immaculate career-woman.'

By the time Sarah returned, Lizzie had assembled the rest of the staff. 'Everyone's here, with the exception of the locum consultant. I'm a bit surprised—he's usually the first to arrive. Perhaps he's been delayed in the traffic. Mind you, it's not quite nine o'clock yet.'

'Well, first of all I'd like to say how pleased

I am to be here and to meet you all. However, I do run a tight ship. I expect excellence from myself and all my staff. Professional conduct at all times.'

Looking around the serious faces, Sarah noted a mixed reaction. Some looked pleased at her words, but there were one or two who shuffled their feet uncomfortably—an older female nurse and one of the plaster-room technicians. She made a mental note to keep an eye on them.

She smiled to soften the impact of her words. 'On the other hand, if anyone has any problems, personal or professional, please, let me know. There's bound to be times when we all need a bit of support.' She saw a couple of staff nodding their heads in agreement.

'I think you'll find me very hands on,' she went on. 'I know some consultants leave a lot to their junior staff, but I like to keep up my clinical skills, so if you have any problems, let me know. Oh, and by the way, I take my coffee black.' Her last comment, spoken lightly, elicited a smile from her colleagues.

As the staff went about their business, Sarah

unclenched her fists, which she had hidden behind her back. She shrugged the tension out of her shoulders. It was important to get off to the right start and it would take time for the team to get to know and trust her. She knew that Dr MacDonald had been in the department for years and was well loved by staff and patients alike. She had been told, however, by the senior managers who had formed part of her interview committee that some of his practices were considered outmoded. She, together with the locum consultant, would be expected to bring the department up to date.

'I'm getting a little long in the tooth for all this,' Dr MacDonald had confided in her when she had gone to see him about the job. 'I find it hard to keep up with the new technology that's sweeping into emergency medicine. I worry sometimes that we depend on it too much. Forget the basic principles of medical practice and lose sight of the patient at the end of all these machines and monitors. Always remember, Dr Carruthers, there is nothing better than your intuition. You strike me as a sensible girl despite your impressive credentials. I'm due to retire about a month after you take up your post, so I'll be there to help in the beginning. After that it will be up to you and whoever replaces me to make the department your own.'

Sarah had been grateful when she'd thought that Dr MacDonald would be around for a while. Regardless of what senior management thought, she knew him to be an excellent consultant with a national reputation. If only she could run the department half as well as he had, she would be happy.

'Come on, then, Dr Carruthers.' Lizzie interrupted her thoughts. 'I'll show you Resus first.'

'Please, Lizzie, except when we're in front of patients, call me Sarah.'

Lizzie showed Sarah around the department. She was pleased to see that everything was immaculate. All the equipment and drugs were stored neatly in the right places and the department was obviously kept well stocked. Lizzie was clearly a woman after her own heart.

'It's quiet so why don't we grab a cup of coffee while we can? I can fill you in on the rest of the information,' Lizzie suggested 'We're lucky enough to have a small staffroom right next to the duty room.'

Lizzie ushered Sarah into the staffroom. Painted in the ubiquitous hospital green, it was simply furnished with a couple of worn arm-chairs and a small coffee-table. A kettle and some mugs rested on top of a small fridge.

But it wasn't the room that caught Sarah's attention. Sitting in one of the armchairs, long legs stretched in front of him, was a figure that made Sarah's heart bang painfully in her chest. Jamie! What on earth was he doing here? The last time Sarah had heard, he had still been in Africa.

Jamie stood up, uncoiling his lean frame. He seemed unsurprised to see her. She caught a flicker of wry amusement in his deep brown eyes.

'Ah, our new consultant,' he drawled in his deep gravelly voice that, to her dismay, still had the power to send shivers up her spine.

'Sarah, may I introduce Dr Jamie Campbell, our locum consultant. He's only been here a couple of weeks, but we're all hoping he'll take Dr MacDonald's job when he officially retires.

Jamie, this is Dr Sarah Carruthers—our new head of department.'

Sarah was speechless. He was the last person she had expected to meet. As Jamie engulfed her hand in his, feelings that she had thought she had managed to suppress came flooding back. He couldn't be here. She wasn't ready.

'Jamie. What brings you to the Royal?' she said, striving to keep her voice even.

'Work.' he said dryly. 'I need to keep my skills up to date, so I agreed to fill in here for a few weeks. But I'm going back to Africa as soon as I can. So, don't worry, whoever gets Dr MacDonald's job, it won't be me.'

Lizzie looked at Sarah, puzzlement furrowing her brow.

'You two know each other?'

'We've worked together before.' Jamie answered before Sarah could respond. 'I guess you could say we know each other pretty well.' He smiled politely, but his eyes were hooded.

'By the way, what happened to you this morning? We missed you at rounds.' Lizzie rushed on, seemingly unaware of the tension between her two colleagues.

Jamie looked a little sheepish. 'I was in early, so I took the opportunity to pop in to see Mrs MacLeod across the road. You remember, the old lady who broke her leg last week? I knew she had been discharged home yesterday and I just wanted to check up on her. She lives alone. And she's a stubborn one. The nurses told me she'd refused home help. I think I've managed to talk her around.'

It was unusual—if not unheard of—for A and E doctors to make house calls. But as Sarah well knew, Jamie had never gone by the book. It was one of the things she loved—*had loved*, she corrected herself—about him. She had known that she would have to see him again, but she'd always imagined that it would be at a time of her choosing. A time when she was prepared, when she could face him cool, calm and collected. Not like this, when he still had the power to set her pulse racing, make her go weak at the knees and, worst of all, send her thoughts spinning in every direction, except the sane, sensible path that she needed to keep him at a distance.

His skin, tanned by the African sun, added to his rugged good looks, making him drop-dead gorgeous. He had changed into theatre greens in preparation for the day ahead and the V of the tunic top revealed the dark crisp hairs on his chest. The trousers were too short for his tall frame, stopping just above his ankles, the thin fabric clinging to the muscles of his legs and hugging his hips. Images of being held in his strong arms, her head against his muscular chest, came rushing back. He was still the most disgustingly attractive man Sarah had ever met.

Before Sarah could think of anything to say, a nurse rushed in. 'Ambulance Control has just phoned. Multiple RTA—ETA five minutes.'

Sarah felt a jolt of adrenaline at the familiar words. Ambulances would be bringing in the casualties from a multiple traffic accident to the department within five minutes. Thinking about Jamie would have to wait.

'How many casualties are we expecting?'

'Three, the two drivers and one of the passengers—a child of about five.'

'OK everyone, let's get ready. Lizzie, could you let theatre know that we might need an emergency theatre? After you've done that, meet me at the entrance.' Jamie was already moving. His laconic manner had disappeared, replaced with an intensity that Sarah knew well. Despite the turmoil he had raised within her, she was glad that he would be working beside her for her first real challenge as a consultant. Whatever else she might feel about him—*And what would that be?* a small voice whispered—Sarah knew that Jamie was one of the best A and E doctors around.

As Sarah and Jamie stood waiting for the casualties to arrive, Sarah turned to Jamie. 'I had no idea you were back in the country.'

'And I had no idea until a few days ago that you had been appointed as the new consultant here. If I'd known, I wouldn't have taken the post. Well done, by the way. I know it's what you always wanted.'

I wanted you, she thought bitterly. She was

dismayed to find how much his words hurt. 'I'm sure we can both manage to put the past behind us,' she said briskly. And then she thought of Calum. God—Calum. Jamie had no idea. How could they possibly put the past behind them?

'We need to talk.'

Jamie narrowed his eyes. 'I thought we had said everything that had to be said. But, sure. Name your time and place.'

The loud wail of sirens signalled the arrival of the road traffic victims, cutting off any further opportunity for discussion.

As the paramedics opened the doors of the ambulances, Jamie and Sarah swung into action. Sarah took the first ambulance, leaving Jamie and Lizzie the remaining two. Lying on a stretcher was a pale woman in her early thirties. She was unconscious. She had a large wound in her forehead which had bled copiously.

While Sarah bent to examine the patient, the paramedic rattled off all the information he had. 'This is the driver of one of the cars. Her son was with her. He's in one of the other ambulances. She's been unconscious but breathing on her own, Glasgow coma scale of 7. Head wound looks superficial but she obviously hit her head quite hard—it was an older car so no airbag. She also has a broken leg. Not sure of other injuries. Pulse is 110 and blood pressure 110 over 50. Oh, and as you can see, she's pregnant. Pretty far on, by the look of things.'

'OK let's get her into Resus.' Sarah turned to one of the junior doctors she had been introduced to earlier. 'Dr Thompson, could you take her in? I'll be with you in just a tick, once I've assessed the other casualties.'

Sarah moved over to the other ambulances. The other driver, an elderly man in his seventies, was sitting up on his trolley, his face covered with an oxygen mask. Lizzie was talking to him reassuringly. She looked up as Sarah approached.

'Mr James here is complaining of chest pain, but he doesn't seem to have any injuries. I'm just taking him into Resus as a precaution. Jamie has already taken the child through.'

Sarah bent over Mr James and listened to his

chest. 'Thanks, Lizzie. Could you organise an ECG? I'll be along in a minute.'

Sarah hurried inside to join her patient. She passed Jamie examining a small child in one of the cubicles. The child was distressed but conscious. Jamie looked up. 'Neil here is fine. A bit shaken, but no damage done. His car seat kept him well protected. We'll just keep him under observation for an hour or two. He said his mummy fell asleep, but that's all I can get out of him so far. Except for a name—Lucy Croy. Do you need any help?'

'Yes, please. If you feel Neil will be OK for the time being with the nursing staff? I could use you in Resus.'

'I'll be back just as soon as I can, Neil.' Jamie said soothingly. 'I'm just going to check up on your mum. Nurse Winter here will look after you. She's got a little boy of just your age.'

As Jamie walked with Sarah she filled him in on the condition of the two other accident victims.

The resus room was a hive of activity when they entered. Doctors and nurses surrounded the two patients, taking blood and setting up drips. Although the air of tension in the room was palpable, everyone was working calmly and efficiently. Mr James had been connected to an ECG machine, which was checking his heart rhythm. One of the junior doctors, a cheerful-looking woman in her mid-twenties who had been introduced to Sarah as Dr Karen Davidson, looked up.

'I'll have the results of his ECG in a few moments and have also taken blood to check his troponin level.'

As one, Jamie and Sarah decided to concentrate on Lucy, who appeared to have regained consciousness but was thrashing around confused.

'We've started a drip on this lady. We've taken blood and urine samples. I've rung Obstetrics and they're sending someone down. Any clue as to what happened?' Dr Thompson asked.

'All we know so far is what the son has told us. He said she fell asleep, but whether he means before the accident or after is unclear. He said her name is Lucy, Lucy Croy,' Jamie replied.

'My son, is he OK? Please, I need to see him.'

Lucy's eyes darted around the room, searching for her little boy. She tried to sit up. Gently Sarah pressed her back onto the trolley.

'Just relax. Neil is absolutely fine. You can see him shortly. But first we need to check you over. Can you remember what happened?'

'Not really. No. Nothing until I woke up here. My baby—is my baby OK?' Lucy clutched her abdomen.

Lizzie bent over Lucy, using the Doptone to search for the baby's heartbeat. She glanced up at Sarah. 'Baby's heartbeat seems fine. But I think we should get Lucy attached to a foetal monitor to be on the safe side.'

'Good idea.' She looked enquiringly at Jamie, who had been examining Lucy's head wound.

'Seems superficial, although it's bled quite a lot. I'd be surprised if it's serious enough to have caused the loss of consciousness, though. We'll get a head CT just to be sure.'

'Dr Carruthers, I have the results of Mr James's tests, if you have a moment,' Dr Davidson called over.

'You go on. We're fine here.' Jamie said.

'We'll know more once we get the blood and urine results.'

Sarah introduced herself to the elderly man lying on the trolley.

'I'm just going to examine you, Mr James. Can you tell me how you're feeling?'

'It's Bill,' he gasped, clearly in some pain. 'I'm all right—a little groggy perhaps. But my chest. It's awfully sore.'

He didn't appear to have any chest injury—she'd checked for bruising or chest tenderness automatically in her rapid but thorough initial assessment.

'Please—could somebody phone my wife? She'll be worried sick. I was only going to the garage to get some petrol. She'd have expected me to be back a long time ago.' Bill was clearly getting increasingly anxious. He struggled to get off the trolley. 'I need to be getting back...'

'Please, Mr James—Bill—try and relax. We'll let your wife know where you are,' Sarah said reassuringly.

She nodded to Dr Davidson. 'Could you ask

one of the nursing staff to try and reach Mrs James? I'd just like to re-examine Bill.'

Sarah's brow furrowed as she reviewed Mr James's ECG. She was at a loss to explain his chest pain. He was a little muddled and was unable to give a clear account of the accident. She fully expected the ECG to show ischaemic changes and was baffled when it appeared normal. But the old man continued to complain of severe chest pain. His blood pressure was low, where she would have expected it to be higher. Karen was looking to her to explain the symptoms, but she couldn't. It was her first real test as a consultant and she was scared she was going to fail it. If only Dr MacDonald were here! She looked up from studying Mr James's X-ray to find Jamie at her elbow.

'Problems?' he asked quietly. Jamie had always been protective of her, right through medical school and beyond. It was on the tip of her tongue to retort that she was managing just fine. It was *she* who was the senior doctor after all! But she knew her reaction was more likely a response to his proximity. Although she wanted nothing more than to put a million miles between them again, Sarah was too much of a professional to ever let personal feelings get in the way of patient care. And, she admitted to herself, there was no one whose medical opinion she trusted more than Jamie's.

'His symptoms don't quite fit. I've looked at his ECG and there isn't anything I wouldn't expect in someone of his age.'

'OK if I examine him?'

'Please. I need all the help I can get.'

Jamie returned a few minutes later, looking worried. 'You're right, it is puzzling, but I have come across something like it once before. I can't be sure, though, until I see his chest X-ray.'

'I've got it up here.'

As Jamie moved closer to scrutinise the X-ray, he brushed against her. Sarah felt an electric shock go through her body that made her toes curl.

'Tell me what you see,' Jamie prompted.

Sarah studied the X-ray for a few moments. 'His aorta seems a little wider than I would have expected—but I can't be sure.'

'That's what I thought,' agreed Jamie. 'But it would be helpful to know if it's always been like that or whether this is something new.'

'Hey, doesn't the department have a computer link with Radiology?' Sarah said.

'Good thinking. We should be able to compare this with any previous X-ray films.' Jamie and Sarah grinned at each other and she felt the past drift away. God, it felt good to be working with Jamie again. *Just that?* The treacherous inner voice was back.

Sarah called Lizzie over, who confirmed that they were able to do what she had asked. Minutes later Mr James's previous X-rays were displayed on the computer screen.

'Bingo!' Sarah exclaimed. 'There, you can see that his aorta is definitely wider than before. Looks like it's ruptured. That would explain his symptoms. We'd better get someone from Cardio. The sooner he's taken to Theatre the better. Could you page for someone, Lizzie? And let Theatre know?' She turned to Jamie and saw her delight mirrored in his eyes.

'Well spotted,' he said warmly.

'Team effort.' she replied sincerely

'We always did make a good team, didn't we?'

Jamie's words hung in the air. Although she knew that he could be referring to when they had been trainees together, the look in his eyes told her that he meant something quite different.

'Jamie, I…' she started to say just as the cardiothoracic consultant, with an entourage of students, rushed in.

'I believe you've got a damaged aorta for me?'

'I'll leave you to it while I check up on Mrs. Croy, shall I?' Jamie dropped one eye in a slow wink before walking away.

'We're pretty certain.' Quickly and concisely Sarah explained Mr James's history.

'You're absolutely right,' the surgeon congratulated her. 'Well picked up. It's a pretty subtle sign on the X-ray and quite often gets missed until the patient's collapsed.'

'I wouldn't have picked it up without Dr Campbell suggesting it might be a possibility. It's not something I've ever come across. Luckily he had once before.'

Once Bill had been taken up to Theatre, Sarah returned to Lucy's bedside.

'She'll be going up to X-Ray soon,' Jamie informed Sarah. 'In the meantime, we'll keep her under close observation.' One of the nursing staff had brought Neil in to see her and he was sitting quietly, holding his mother's hand and watching the activity in the room with wide-eyed interest. Lucy seemed a lot calmer now that she had her son by her side. Sarah stretched to ease the kinks in her back.

'Well done, everyone. Great work.' Sarah glanced at her watch. 'Good grief, is that the time?' Hours had passed since the ambulances had arrived and Sarah was suddenly conscious of feeling ravenous. Besides, she wanted to check on Calum. 'If you guys want to go for lunch, I'll man the fort until you come back.'

Jamie eyed Sarah. She was still as beautiful as he remembered in a delicate way that belied the iron resolve he knew underpinned everything she did. She looked tired, dark circles bruised the delicate skin under her eyes. But despite the tiredness there was a new fullness to her breasts and roundness to her cheeks that hadn't been there before. At one time he had known every inch of her body and these curves were most definitely new. Nice, but new. He longed to run his hands over her body to refamiliarise himself with her contours. Damn it! He wanted to do more than that, he admitted to himself.

'I had a huge breakfast,' he said, patting his lean abdomen. 'I'm quite happy to wait an hour or so. Why don't you go with Lizzie? She can continue filling you in about the department while I check at Reception and deal with any waiting patients.'

'No, you and Sarah go, Jamie.' Lizzie suggested. 'I've checked and there's nobody waiting to see a doctor just now. I'll stay with Lucy. Besides, I'm on a diet,' she said, indicating her curves. 'Need to get into my dress for the wedding so I brought a salad. I can always page you if I need you. Go on the pair of you—shoo.'

Sarah didn't feel ready to be alone with Jamie. There were things she needed to tell him, but she wanted to be away from the distractions of the hospital so they could talk without interruption. Furthermore, she couldn't think clearly in his presence. She desperately wanted time alone to gather her thoughts.

And her feet were killing her. The new shoes she hadn't been able to resist to go with her new suit were rubbing painfully. She'd forgotten what it was like to be constantly on your feet. It would be comfortable if unfashionable shoes from now on, she promised herself. She flicked off one high-heeled shoe and rubbed her sore toes on the back of a trousered leg.

'I'm quite happy to put my feet up for a few moments in the staffroom with a cup of coffee.'

But Jamie clearly had other ideas. 'You need to eat.' he said firmly. 'I'll go to the canteen and get some sandwiches—you put the kettle on. Then you can put your feet up while you're eating. There's a spare pair of theatre sandals in the cupboard if you like.'

Good grief, did nothing escape the man? Sore feet or not, nothing would persuade her to clump around in theatre sandals. She glared at Jamie, making it clear that she found his suggestion preposterous. Noting the twinkle in Jamie's eyes, she smiled ruefully. He obviously remembered the fetish she had always had for shoes.

'You win. Five minutes in the staffroom?'

Sarah filled the kettle and set out the mugs for coffee before reaching for the phone. Although she had promised not to call, she couldn't help herself. She just had to check that Calum wasn't upset and crying for her.

As she waited for the call to be answered, Jamie arrived back with a pile of sandwiches and some fruit, which he dumped on the coffee-table.

'There, that should see us through the next few hours,' he said. 'Sorry, I didn't notice you were on the phone.'

'There's no answer,' Sarah replied, replacing the receiver, small lines of anxiety creasing her brow. Could Calum be sick? Had her mother taken him to the doctor? Don't be silly, she admonished herself. Perhaps they'd gone for a walk or her mother was changing Calum and couldn't come to the phone. There could be a hundred reasons. That didn't stop her from worrying, however.

'Is anything wrong?' Jamie asked, as ever tuned into her moods.

'My mother isn't answering the phone.'

'Is that a problem? Is she ill?' Jamie had met Sarah's mother often and the last he'd known she had been in the best of health. Still, she was getting older and it had been a long time since he had last seen her.

'No it's not that. It's…' Sarah tailed off.

Jamie looked at her quizzically, cocking an eyebrow.

Just as Sarah was formulating the words to tell Jamie about Calum, there was a soft tap on the door and one of the male nurses popped his head into the room.

'Visitor, or should I say visitors, for you, Dr Carruthers. And can I just say he's absolutely gorgeous.' He stepped back, allowing Sarah's mother, with Calum in her arms, to enter.

'Mum! What is it? Is Calum all right?' Sarah said anxiously, reaching for her son. But it was immediately apparent from the smiles and gurgles as big brown eyes gazed into hers adoringly that her child was in perfect health.

'We were out for a walk, so I thought we'd just step in for a moment and say hello. We'd have crept away without disturbing you if you'd been busy. But I thought it would put your mind at rest if you could see for yourself how perfectly content Calum is.'

Catching sight of Jamie, Sarah's mother's lips formed a large O. 'Well, I never! Jamie. I must say I didn't expect to find you here.' She looked from Sarah to Jamie, perplexed.

For a moment Sarah froze. In her anxiety for her son, she had completely forgotten about Jamie's presence. She resisted the desire to grab her son and bolt from the room. Anything to put off the moment when she'd have to tell him. She sneaked a look at Jamie, who was looking confused. 'Jamie is the locum consultant here, Mum. He started a few weeks ago. Jamie, this is Calum, my son.'

'Your son!' Jamie said disbelievingly. Well, why not? He hadn't expected her to live the life of a nun. Heaven knew, *he* hadn't. But he hadn't expected her to find someone else so soon. Had she been that desperate to have children? How old was the child? Around six months, he guessed, although he was no expert. He started doing some mental arithmetic in his head. That meant she must have fallen pregnant soon after he'd left. That *was* quick.

Sarah busied herself pouring coffee. She turned her back on Jamie, taking a few deep breaths to steady her nerves. The teacup rattled in the saucer.

'Mama.' Calum gave a plaintive cry, reaching once more for his mother.

'You take your child. I'll get the coffee,' Jamie offered. Sarah scooped Calum into her arms. She covered his face with kisses, murmuring soothing endearments until he stopped fretting. Calum turned his wide brown eyes on Jamie. He had seen those eyes before. Then suddenly it hit him. Those were the same eyes he saw in the mirror every morning when he shaved.

Sarah stole a glance at Jamie. The colour had drained from his face as he looked from her to Calum. His lips tightened and his eyes were as grim as she had ever seen them. She felt the blood run cold in her veins. Not just angry she thought—furious.

'Mrs Carruthers, could you excuse us, please?' Jamie said, a river of steel running through his voice. 'I think Sarah and I have to talk.'

CHAPTER TWO

'WE DO have to talk, Jamie, but this is not the time or the place.' Sarah said, unwrapping the small arms from around her neck. 'Mum, could you take Calum home now, please?'

Mrs Carruthers moved to take Calum from his mother's arms but the baby, sensing the tension in the room, clung tighter to his mother.

'I'll just step out for a minute, shall I?' Calum's grandmother said, beating a hasty retreat and closing the door behind her.

'You had no right.' Jamie's eyes were almost black with fury—and something else. Could it be fear? wondered Sarah. Was he *that* terrified of becoming a father? Well, he needn't worry. She and Calum had managed just fine without him and would continue to manage without him. Or so she tried to convince herself, deliberately forcing back the memories of the lonely nights when she had longed for his strong body next to hers, his comforting arms around her, sharing the joys and anxieties of parenthood as well as her bed.

'It is nothing to do with you, Jamie. You made it perfectly clear that you didn't want children—or me, for that matter.' Sarah fought hard to keep her voice steady. She had no intention of letting him know how much he had hurt her when he had left.

'Were you ever going to let me know?'

'Let you know what exactly?'

'That I had fathered a child.'

'Are you so sure that it's yours?' Sarah bit back, and then immediately regretted the words. Of course he had to know Calum was his. Despite the fact he had made it clear that he never wanted children, he did have the right to know. Even if he wanted nothing to do with either of them.

'Not mine?' For a moment hope flared in his deep brown eyes. Sarah felt as if her heart had been squeezed.

Jamie strode towards her, his mouth set in a

grim line. Involuntarily, Sarah stepped back, hugging Calum protectively. Jamie shot her a look of questioning anguish before gently moving aside the blanket covering the small body. The baby gazed up at him with solemn brown eyes. A tiny hand reached out and wrapped itself around one of Jamie's fingers. The child pulled the finger into his mouth and gnawed with the nub of a tooth. Jamie's heart lurched. He felt ill.

'Oh, Sarah, what *have* you done?' he said, his voice edged with despair.

Sarah had imagined this moment for months. But never quite like this. In the small hours of the night, when she had lain in her big empty bed almost overwhelmed with the responsibility for the small life that depended so utterly on her, she'd imagined Jamie coming back into her life and, if not loving her, at least loving his child. She had never expected, or wanted, his financial help—she earned enough to provide quite comfortably for her and her child—but Calum needed a father figure. Someone who would play football with him, take him fishing, all the things that she imagined other fathers did.

'It's not just what *I* did, Jamie. You of all people should know that it takes two to make a baby,' she said, a small smile twisting her mouth.

Jamie had removed himself to the other side of the room, putting as much physical distance as possible between him and Sarah and the baby. He looked at her coldly. 'You told me you were on the Pill,' Jamie said flatly. 'I would never…'

'Never what, Jamie? Made love to me? If I remember correctly, that last night when you came round, you couldn't wait to get me back in your bed.'

Sarah's cheeks burned at the memory of their last night together. Of him standing in her small sitting room, looking as beautiful and dangerously enticing as Lucifer. Of her capitulation and their frenzied love-making before he had left her in the early hours of the morning. She had woken to find him staring down at her. Had it been a trick of the moonlight that had made her imagine the tenderness in his eyes as he'd gazed down at her? She had reached up and pulled him towards her. 'I could come with you,' she had whispered, not caring that she was laying her heart at his feet. He had gently detached her hands from around his neck.

'You are about to achieve everything you ever dreamed of in your career, Sarah. I can't give you what you want from me. Not when I'm…' He had hesitated. 'Not the committing kind.' And so he had left with one last lingering kiss.

Sarah forced her thoughts back to the present.

'And I *was* on the Pill,' she stressed 'until you told me it was over between us. And I thought it really was. That last evening was, well, unexpected.' Once more her cheeks flared as she stumbled over her words. Calum was getting restless in his mother's arms, beginning to squirm.

'Why didn't you tell me when you found out you were pregnant?' Sarah winced as Jamie ground out the words. 'Didn't you think I had the right to know?' He stood, arms crossed, looking at Sarah. She had seen that look before, usually when he had been justifiably ticking off some junior doctor for failing in some way. It was the first time she had ever had his disapproval directed at her. She lifted her chin.

'And what would you have done?' she asked scathingly 'Come rushing back? Offered to make an honest woman of me? No, Jamie. You made it crystal clear that marriage and children weren't part of your plans.'

'You could have had a termination.' Jamie's voice was emotionless. Sarah felt as if she had been kicked in the stomach.

'A termination? Oh, believe me, I thought about it. I wasn't ready to be a mum. And certainly not a single mother. But when it came down to it I just couldn't do it. She clutched Calum closer, unable to imagine a life without him. 'Is that what you would have wanted me to do? How can you bear to think that? Especially now that you've seen him? No, Jamie, having Calum was the best decision I ever made in my life. If you feel differently, I was right not to tell you.'

Jamie rubbed his face tiredly. Suddenly all the anger seemed to drain out of him.

'You don't understand...' he began, but

before he could finish there was an urgent rap at the door and Lizzie pushed the door open.

'Jamie, Sarah, sorry to interrupt,' she said, taking in the atmosphere in the room with a quizzical eye, 'but I'm a bit worried about Mrs Croy—the pregnant lady.'

Jamie and Sarah immediately focused their attention on the young nurse, following her out of the room towards Resus.

'Could you take Calum home, Mum?' Sarah said as she passed her mother in the corridor. Calum immediately let out a loud wail at being removed from his mother's arms and Sarah couldn't suppress the pang she felt as she passed him over.

'I can handle this,' Jamie said tightly.

'I know you can, but it's my job, too. Calum will be fine in a moment.'

'Are you sure?' Jamie asked, his voice softening. But Sarah was already striding off in front of him without a backward glance at her snuffling baby. Surreptitiously she blinked back the tears that threatened to fall. She was determined not to let anyone see, least of all Jamie, how much Calum's cries tore at her heart. Millions of women had to leave their babies to work. As she had told Jamie, she had a job to do.

Her baby's plaintive cries still ringing in her ears, she bent over the frightened woman lying on the gurney in front of her.

Lucy looked from Sarah to Jamie, her eyes full of terror.

'I haven't felt my baby move since I came in. That's not normal, is it?' She reached over and clutched Jamie's arm with a strength that her small frame belied. 'Please, Doctor, don't let anything happen to my baby.'

'Try not to worry,' Jamie said softly. 'We're going to do everything in our power to make sure your baby stays healthy.'

'The obstetrician was down earlier, but thought everything was fine. He was happy for Mrs Croy to stay in the department while she had all her tests. We kept the monitor on, though, as he suggested,' Lizzie told the doctors. Sarah could read the anxiety in her eyes. Clearly she felt something was wrong, too.

'Could I see the tracing?' Sarah asked. It had

been a long time since she had done obstetrics and she prayed she remembered enough.

Lizzie handed Sarah the tracing of the baby's heartbeat. The lines looked ominously flat, suggesting the baby was in some distress. Wordlessly she passed it to Jamie. 'Get the obstetrican back down here stat, please, Lizzie. As well as a paediatrician and anaesthetist,' she added quietly, not wishing to further alarm the already terrified mother.

Jamie looked at the tracing and nodded at Sarah.

'I'd just like to have another look at your tummy if I may, Lucy.'

Jamie lifted Lucy's gown and felt her abdomen. 'Her abdomen feels soft and normal but…' He stepped back, looking puzzled for a moment. 'Sarah, what do you make of this?' Sarah bent over the woman. She could just make out a line of discolouration underneath Lucy's swollen abdomen.

'It looks like bruising from the seat belt.'

Jamie nodded grimly.

'It wasn't here when I first examined her. But

bruising can take an hour or two to develop.'
Sarah knew immediately what was causing his
frown of concern.

'Lucy, I just want to examine you down below.'

Lucy's frantic eyes darted from Jamie to
Sarah. It was clear she could sense their concern.

'She has some bleeding.' Sarah finished examining Lucy and looked at Jamie. She read the
confirmation in his eyes.

'Lucy,' Jamie said gently, 'we think you
might have had an abruption. It's where the
placenta—the bit that nourishes the baby—
breaks away from the wall of the uterus. It
means we are going to have to get your baby
delivered straight away.'

'Is my baby going to die?' Lucy whispered.

'Not if we've got anything to do with it. We're
going to have to perform a Caesarean section
and get the baby out. Lizzie, could you set up
Resus for the op?'

Damn, where was the obstetrician? Sarah
thought. It had been a few years since she had
done a section. As an accident and emergency
trainee she had been taught how to do it for emer-

gencies such as this. But it had always been under the supervision of a consultant obstetrician.

Jamie caught her look and smiled reassuringly as he started scrubbing up. He seemed to read her mind. 'We don't have time to wait. Hopefully Donald will be here shortly, but I've done dozens of C-sections in Africa. We didn't have the luxury of obstetricians in the hospital I worked in, so we all had plenty of practice. How do you feel about assisting?'

'Like a hole in the head,' Sarah muttered under her breath. Some first day! Could it possibly get any worse? But she couldn't let her anxiety show. Not when everyone was watching her closely. 'Of course I'm happy to assist.'

'Better still, why don't you do it and I'll talk you through it?' Jamie suggested.

He was right, of course. It would be a good way for her to brush up on her technique while having someone experienced standing by. She had always loved the surgical part of her training, taking pride in her neat needlework.

His confidence in her helped her make up her mind. 'OK. Lizzie, could you call in the medical staff who are free to observe?' It would be good experience for them. They were part of a teaching hospital after all. Part of the consultants' responsibilities was to ensure that junior medical staff got thorough training in all aspects of emergency medicine. She looked at Lucy, who had been listening in, clearly terrified.

'Do we have your permission, Lucy?' she asked gently. 'It really is necessary to get baby out as soon as possible.'

Lucy looked from Sarah to Jamie for a moment before making up her mind. Mutely, she nodded her agreement. 'Just save my baby,' she pleaded.

Within minutes the young mother was draped and the staff gowned up. The anaesthetist arrived and gave her a spinal anaesthetic to deaden the feeling below her waist. The medical and nursing staff stood around to observe. Sarah knew they'd be interested to see how their new boss coped with the emergency.

Sarah took the scalpel Jamie held out for her and made a neat incision across Lucy's abdomen roughly where the seat belt had caused the bruising. Jamie used his hands to hold the layers of muscle and fat so that Sarah could see more easily what she was doing. Just as she made the final incision into the uterus, the obstetrician, Donald, appeared gowned and gloved.

'Sorry, folks. It's bedlam upstairs. Everything was perfectly quiet until an hour ago then all hell broke loose…' He watched Sarah for a few moments. 'Looks like you've got everything under control here. Are you OK to close up or would you like me to hang around? It's just that they could do with my help upstairs and you guys seem to be handling everything here.'

Almost before he had finished speaking, Sarah removed the baby, nodding her agreement to the harassed obstetrician while smiling her pleasure at the new arrival. Jamie checked the baby was starting to breathe as he prepared to cut the cord. 'You have a beautiful, healthy baby girl Lucy. You have a quick hold of her and then we'll let the paediatrician give her a quick once-over while Dr Carruthers stitches you up.'

He turned to Donald. 'It's all right. You can

go. We'll finish up here then get Mrs Croy and baby up to the postnatal ward.'

Jamie watched as Sarah stitched Mrs Croy's abdomen together, her small hands working quickly. Unbidden, the image of those same hands fluttering across his chest and moving downwards rushed back. She had always had the power to surprise him. Underneath that cool professional exterior was a woman of hidden passion and innovation. At the memory he almost groaned aloud. Ye gods, he thought to himself, he had to concentrate on work. Seeing he was no longer required, he quietly left the room.

Later, Jamie went in search of the solitude of the staffroom. He needed time to think. He had managed to avoid being alone with Sarah for the rest of the shift. It hadn't been difficult. By the time Mrs Croy had been taken up to the postnatal ward, a queue of non-urgent patients had formed and he and all the other doctors had had to work flat out to ensure that they were all seen and treated.

But by six in the evening all the patients requiring the consultants' expertise had either been sent home or dispatched to the wards for follow-up care. Most of the junior day medical staff had gone, replaced by the night shift.

He was pretty certain that Sarah had left for the day. The full implications of seeing her again and finding out that she had a son—*they* had a son—had hit him hard. But now wasn't the time for rational discussion. Not before he knew exactly what he was going to do.

To his dismay, when he opened the door to the staffroom, he found Sarah sitting in one of the armchairs, holding a cup of coffee loosely in her hands. Her head was leaning back, exposing her long, delicate neck, and her eyes were closed, her breathing steady. Her thick blonde hair had come loose from the rather severe chignon she'd had when she'd arrived that morning and fell in wisps about her face. It made her look younger than her twenty-nine years and very vulnerable. As he watched her sleeping form he realised that despite the fifteen months and the continents that had he had put between them, he still cared for her. His heart twisted. How would she feel when she knew the truth? And one way or another, eventually she would have to know

'SJ?' he said quietly as he reached forward and gently removed the mug from her fingers, unsure if she was asleep. Her eyes fluttered open and for a long moment her green eyes, heavily fringed with dark lashes, gazed into his.

'Jamie,' she murmured dreamily.

Then suddenly she sprang to her feet.

'How long have you been watching me?'

'I've just come in. I thought you'd be long gone by now. Don't you have someone you need to get home to?' he said gently.

'Calum! He'll be waiting for me.' She looked at her watch. 'Is that the time already? It'll be his bedtime soon,' she said wistfully.

'Off you go. I'll finish up here,' Jamie offered

'I won't be treated any differently. I am fully prepared to take my share of the workload. I'll go home when I'm good and ready,' she told him, eyes flashing. But Jamie could see the fatigue in the deepening circles around her eyes and the way she moved to try and ease her aching back. Before he could stop himself he came up behind her and started massaging her shoulders with strong fingers.

He felt a shudder go through her slight frame and for a moment she leaned against him. He breathed in the heady scent of her perfume and the fragrance of her shampoo. He felt himself grow hard at the memories the feel of her body evoked. Aghast, he pushed her away from him.

She looked at him, confusion in her emerald green eyes.

'Go home, Sarah,' he said huskily.

'I need to write up some notes before I can leave,' she responded tiredly.

'Leave them. I'll do them. Now, go home, woman, before I lift you bodily out of this department.' It wasn't the right thing to say. For a moment he detected a glint of rebellion in her eyes before the shutters came down.

She held her hands up. 'OK. OK, I'm going!' she said, slipping a note in his hand before she left. 'My new address and telephone number. We will have to talk some time, but preferably not in the hospital.'

After Sarah left, Jamie sank back into the chair, still warm from Sarah's body, his head in his hands. Why couldn't he have stayed away from her that last night?

He had been a fool. A selfish fool. Now everything had changed. With a sigh he picked up the phone.

'Robert? Jamie,' he said when the phone was answered. 'Look, I need a favour from you. Never mind what it is right now, but could you come around to my flat, say, about eight this evening? Great I'll fill you in then.' He replaced the receiver. There was one thing he still had to do before he left for the night. He left the staffroom and made his way to the nurses' station. Checking to make sure that there was no one around, he selected a couple of needles, syringes and vials for collecting blood, and slipped them into his pocket.

Sarah moved around the kitchen, putting laundry away and making up the next day's bottles. It had taken longer than usual to settle Calum, who had been fractious and unsettled after a day without his mother. She was exhausted. It had not been a good first day, she thought. Oh, the work had been demanding, but she had loved every minute of it. She supposed practising medicine was like riding a bike—you never really forgot what to do. And as long as you kept up with the latest medical journals… She cast a guilty eye at the unread pile sitting on her coffee-table.

No, it wasn't work that had left her feeling as if she had done a few rounds with a heavy weight boxer, it had been meeting Jamie again on top of the emotional upheaval of leaving Calum. Her son and her job was as much as she could cope with right now. The last thing she needed, in her already over-complicated life, was Jamie Campbell stirring up old emotions.

'You should go to bed, darling,' her mother said, entering the kitchen. She, too, looked tired. Something else to feel guilty about. Her mother wasn't getting any younger and, God knew, looking after a six-month-old baby for hours at a time clearly took its toll.

'No, you get yourself home, Mum. I'm fine. Besides…'

'You're hoping he'll phone or call round, aren't you?' her mother said softly. 'But it's almost ten, so it's a little unlikely, don't you think?'

'Why didn't he let me know he was back? I could have broken the news better.'

'I thought you decided you weren't going to tell him?'

'I wasn't. There didn't seem to be a need. I thought if he knew, guilt—or a sense of duty—would make him try to pick up where we left off—he's that kind of man. But it wouldn't be because of me. It would be because of Calum. And I don't want him unless…' Calum stirred in his sleep. Mrs Carruthers followed Sarah into the nursery. They both held their breath as Calum sighed and his breathing grew deep and regular once more. The two women stood over the sleeping form and smiled at each other.

'Unless he can love you, too. Not just because you are the mother of his child,' her mother finished for her.

'Something like that, I guess.' Sarah grinned

wryly. 'But we can manage, can't we? I have Calum, you and my career. It's enough. There's no room in my life for a love affair. When would I have the time?' She laughed but there was a break in her voice. 'Anyway,' Sarah went on, 'he clearly wasn't lying when he told me he didn't want children. Did you see his reaction when he realised Calum was his? I know he said he didn't want children, but surely after seeing Calum he must feel something? Oh, Mum, how can he not care? What will I tell Calum when he's older? How can I tell him his father didn't want him—even when he knew about him? Why did he have to come back? We were fine as we were.'

'It'll have been a shock for Jamie,' her mother said placatingly. 'After all, you had almost nine months to get used to the fact you were going to be a mother.'

'You always did defend him,' Sarah replied, hurt.

'I'm not defending him. How could I defend any man who hurt my only daughter as badly as he hurt you? You're better off without him,

Sarah. One day you'll find someone to love you who is worthy of you. Someone who'll love Calum as if he were his own.'

'I don't want anyone else. I mean…I don't want anyone. I'm never going to let a man get under my skin again. Least of all Jamie Campbell. And I certainly don't want Calum to have a father who flits in and out of his life, like mine did. Never knowing if or when he'd turn up…'

And usually he hadn't. Sarah winced at the memories of her childhood self, sitting waiting eagerly for her father to take her out for the day. She would have been up for hours, getting dressed in her best dress, hair neatly brushed, almost giddy with excitement. And then, as the hours had passed, she had gradually given up hope until at last she had gone to bed to sob her eight-year-old heart out.

Jean Carruthers looked at her daughter sadly. 'I'm so sorry, Sarah. Your father was a weak man. But…' she shook her head in puzzlement '…Jamie Campbell never struck me as being weak.' She pulled on her coat ready to leave.

'Weak—no. Selfish? Perhaps. Whatever. He

has no place in our lives.' Sarah wondered just who she was trying so hard to convince. She kissed her mother goodbye. 'Unfortunately we have to work together until he returns to Africa. I have to be professional about this, but the sooner he goes back, the happier I'll be.'

Jamie placed the tourniquet just above his elbow. Using his teeth, he pulled on one end to make it tight. He tapped at a swollen vein with a finger before inserting the needle. Blood rushed into the tube. As he released the tourniquet there was knock on the door. Jamie carefully placed the vial to one side before answering it. Robert stood there, right on time.

The two men exchanged small talk while Jamie poured them two large measures of malt whiskey.

'You didn't ask me over here to talk pleasantries,' Robert said astutely.

'No.' Jamie admitted. Then he quickly explained what he wanted Robert to do and why.

When he had finished, Robert looked thoughtful.

'I had no idea. You never told anyone, did you?'

'There was no reason to. It was nobody's business except mine.'

'Until now.'

'Until now.' Jamie agreed flatly

'I always did wonder why you let her go. We all thought you'd found your match in Sarah Carruthers.'

'I had. That's why I had to let her go. The other women didn't matter. They knew that I wasn't in it for the long term. But Sarah—Sarah was different.'

'Why didn't you tell her? She's a doctor. She would've understood—if she truly loved you.'

'How could I tell her? I'm not the kind of man that would prevent a woman from having the children she wanted. The type of man who would tie a woman to him, to have her look after me. Give up her career, her future. No, I could never ask that of any woman. Least of all Sarah.'

'But you could have had the test before now!' Robert continued to insist.

'No,' Jamie said quietly. 'I decided a long time ago that if I had inherited the disease, I'd rather not know. I'd rather live in the here and now. Live every day as if it might be my last. It's the way I am, Robert, for better or worse.'

'Surely you have to tell Sarah now? She has a right to know.'

'What's the point in telling her now? It's too late. If the test is negative then she'll have spent the time worrying unnecessarily. If it's positive…' Jamie shook his head despairingly. 'Well, of course she'll have to know then.' He stood up, indicating the conversation was at an end. 'But this is getting us nowhere. I appreciate your concern but what I need you to do is to take the blood specimens and expedite them through the system as fast as possible.'

'They normally like you to have counselling in advance of the results,' Robert reminded Jamie as he pocketed the specimens and made for the door.

'It's not counselling I need, Robert. It's answers. Just do your best.'

CHAPTER THREE

SARAH was feeding Calum his breakfast next morning when her mother arrived. They'd had a tug of wills over the teaspoon Sarah was using to feed him. Calum had made several attempts to pull it from Sarah's hand and most of his breakfast had landed in his hair. He was delighted with this new game, smiling up at his mother to reveal a single tooth.

'What am I to do with you? Just as well I haven't had my shower yet.'

Calum responded by kicking his legs out in front of him in delight.

'You'd better jump in the shower, Sarah Jane,' her mother advised, eyeing the gloop that clung to one of Sarah's eyebrows. 'I'll finish feeding this young man if you like. I'll give him a bath after you leave.'

After months of searching, Sarah had managed to find a small house for the three of them near the hospital. It was small, but it had a garden and a small granny flat with a separate entrance for her mother. It meant that her mother could always be close at hand to help, but Sarah was also aware that her mother was getting older and if there came a time when she might need Sarah to help her, she would be able to return the favour.

When Sarah arrived at the hospital, the department was already mobbed with patients, although it wasn't quite eight.

She hadn't slept well. Despite her exhaustion it had taken her a long time to fall asleep. Unsettling thoughts of Jamie had tumbled around her head. She still couldn't quite believe that she'd be working with him, seeing him every day. How would she cope, knowing now that the time apart had done little to diminish the feelings she had for him? She had believed that she had got over him, although the daily sight of her child had been a constant reminder of his father. And if she hadn't been ready to see

Jamie, she had been less prepared for him to find out about Calum. It had all happened too quickly. Could she really blame Jamie for being shocked and dismayed? When she had at last fallen into a restless sleep, it had only been to dream of him. A Jamie who looked at her with angry, disappointed eyes.

She wanted to find out what was happening before the junior doctors arrived for rounds at eight-thirty so she went in search of the night shift. She was unsurprised to find a dark head bent over case notes.

'Oh, hello, so we didn't scare you off?' Jamie said, looking up.

'Of course not. Yesterday was a fairly typical day, wouldn't you say?'

'Not in every aspect, no.' Jamie returned.

'No, er, well, perhaps not,' Sarah had to agree. She supposed, certainly hoped, it wasn't every day that Jamie found out he was the father of a child. 'Anyway, let's get started, shall we?'

'I've already been around. There's nothing that the juniors can't handle. I was about to go up to the wards to see our two from yesterday.

I've already spoken to the medical staff on Postnatal and Cardiology and apparently all three are doing fine.'

'It would have broken Lucy's heart if she'd lost the baby. Do you mind if I come up with you? I'd love to check up on them for myself, as well as see more of the hospital. We don't get to see the positive results of our work, do we? Patch them up and send them home usually.'

Sarah followed Jamie up to four flights of stairs to the labour ward.

'You wait for the lift if you like,' he offered. But Sarah didn't want to appear a wimp. Besides, she thought, thinking of the couple of extra pounds she wanted to lose after giving birth, she could do with the exercise. Exercise was something else she had to add to her to do list!

Jamie waited at the top of the stairs for her to arrive. He looked amused as she tried to disguise her laboured breath. 'Do you still climb?' Climbing and hill walking had been a shared passion. But Sarah had never taken the risks he had. He had seemed to always push himself. It had been as if he'd been driven. He had always looked for more difficult climbs, higher mountains. He had refused point blank to take her along on his more dangerous expeditions. She had argued with him that his attitude was patronising and sexist. But he had refused to be swayed. Sarah knew him to be a stubborn man once he had made up his mind. Just as he had made up his mind that he didn't want her, she thought bitterly.

'I don't exactly have the time!' she retorted. 'What, between a young baby and a full-time job.'

'Of course you don't. Sorry, that was stupid of me.' He flashed her one of his heart-stoppingly gorgeous broad grins and her heart lurched. She felt a surge of desire that warmed her body to the tips of her toes. Damn the man that he could still make her feel like that.

'We really don't know that much about each other, do we?' she replied coolly. 'Do you know which room Mrs Croy is in?' Sarah peeked into the room opposite the nurses' station where the patients recovering from surgery were always put and, sure enough, she could see Lucy sitting up in bed, holding her tiny baby. What she didn't expect to see were the tears that rolled down the young mother's cheeks.

'Perhaps you could let the staff know we're here?' she suggested to Jamie, nodding her head in the direction of the weeping woman. She wanted a few moments alone with Lucy and, besides, it was hospital etiquette to inform staff that visiting medics were present.

She tapped gently on the door. 'Can I come in, Lucy?'

Lucy sniffed away the tears. 'Dr Carruthers. It's good of you to come and see us.' Sarah slipped over to the side of the bed.

'May I?' she said, holding out her arms for the baby.

Wordlessly Lucy passed her daughter to Sarah. Sarah pushed back the blanket wrapping the baby to reveal a tiny face with rosebud lips. Blue eyes fixed on her face for a few seconds before scrunching up as the infant started to wail.

'Oh, dear,' said Sarah, 'I think I've unsettled her.'

'It's not you,' Lucy replied, joining her baby

in loud sobs, 'it's me. She's hungry and I can't get her to feed. I didn't manage to breastfeed Neil,' she hiccuped, 'and I really wanted to feed this baby myself. But I can't.'

'It's not easy these first few days. It took me quite a few goes before I could get the hang of things,' Sarah confided softly.

'You?' Lucy said disbelievingly. 'You look like someone who manages to do everything perfectly first time.' But she looked interested and her tears were beginning to dry up.

Sarah laughed. 'That's just because people think doctors know everything but we don't. We're just the same as everyone else underneath. I promise you, I shed a good few tears when I first tried to feed my baby. But you know what? I had someone who spent quite a bit of time showing me how it was done and sat with me until I felt confident. Would you like me to help you?'

'Could you? I mean, are you sure you're not too busy?'

'Too busy to help a fellow mum? Never. Here, let me help you fix baby on.' Sarah perched on the bed beside Lucy and her infant.

Within a few moments and after only one or two false starts the baby was sucking contentedly at her mother's breast.

Lucy and Sarah smiled at each other. 'There you go! I'll come up later and see how you're getting on.' Sarah noticed Lucy's eyes drift towards the door. She turned around to find Jamie standing there, his expression inscrutable. She had no idea how long he'd been watching them.

'I can see you have your hands full, Mrs Croy,' he said. 'I'll come up and see you another time.' He nodded to Sarah. 'Ready?'

As Sarah and Jamie were about to leave, one of the nursing staff came bustling over. She was small and curvaceous with dark hair tied in a thick plait that fell down her back.

'Jamie, are we still on for tonight?' She touched him on the shoulder with a familiarity that set Sarah's teeth on edge. Was this woman the reason he hadn't called last night? Not that his love life was anything to do with her, she reminded herself.

'Sure. I'm on call, so we can't eat anywhere too far from the hospital.' Jamie slid a look in

Sarah's direction. 'By the way, this is my colleague and the accident and emergency's new head of department, Dr Sarah Carruthers. Sarah, this is Annie Walker, midwife in charge of the postnatal ward.'

Annie looked at Sarah appraisingly. 'Pleased to meet you. Nice work yesterday, by the way. I've never seen such beautiful stitching,' she said warmly. 'Lucy has a lot to thank you and Jamie for.' Annie looked at Jamie with blatant admiration. 'Let's not go out. Why don't I cook and we can have a lazy night in?' Her eyes twinkled, leaving Sarah in no doubt as to the kind of lazy night she had in mind.

'Nice to meet you, but if you'll both excuse me, I have work to do.' If Jamie thought she had nothing better to do than be a witness to his love life then he was much mistaken. 'I'll see you back in the department once I've been to see Mr James.' She was aware she sounded a little frosty, but couldn't help herself.

Jamie glanced at her, amusement warming his eyes. A half-smile played on his lips. 'I'll be along in a minute.'

Grief, he couldn't possibly think she was jealous. Sarah glared at him before turning on her heel.

Mr James was still in Intensive Care, but the nursing staff expected him to be moved out to the cardiology ward in a day or two. His wife, an elderly lady with bright eyes and a shock of white hair, was by his bedside.

'This is Dr Carruthers, Mary.' Mr James's voice was raspy from the tube that he'd had in earlier to help him breathe, and Sarah knew it would take a couple of days for any residual swelling to dissipate. 'She saved my life.'

Mary wrapped Sarah's hands in hers.

'Thank you so much, Doctor. He's a grumpy old so and so, but he's very precious to me.'

'We were only doing our job. But although he seems to be doing well, he's not out of the woods quite yet.' She didn't want to frighten the elderly couple, but a ruptured aorta, serious enough in a younger man, could be devastating in a man of Bill's years. She turned to the old man. 'You had us a little baffled for a while. Luckily for us, Dr

Campbell picked up on your husband's condition in time.'

'Where is that young man of yours? I want to thank him, too.'

'Young man of mine?' Sarah said, puzzled. Just what was he talking about?

'Your young man—the other doctor. We'd like to thank him, too.'

'You mean Dr Campbell?' Sarah laughed nervously. 'He's not my young man. Whatever gave you that idea?'

'I wasn't so out of it that I didn't notice the way he was looking at you,' Bill insisted. Sarah felt her cheeks redden.

'Shush Bill,' his wife cautioned. 'You're embarrassing the young doctor. I'm sure she doesn't want to discuss her personal life with an old fool like you.' Despite the words, Sarah could see the very real love that existed between the couple. She sighed. Some people were so lucky. To find love and be able to hang onto it.

'How long have you two been married?'

'Fifty years.' Mary smiled at her husband 'And it seems like yesterday. When you meet the right one, dear, you hang on to him for all you're worth. Real love doesn't come along more than once. I almost lost my Bill during the war. If he hadn't come back to me, that would have been it. I would never have married anyone else.'

Bill looked over Sarah's shoulder. 'Oh, here he is. Your young man.'

Jamie raised a quizzical eyebrow as he entered the room. 'Whose young man?'

Really, the man had the most annoying habit of arriving at the most inopportune moments! Sarah thought irritably.

'I can assure you both that while Dr Campbell has plenty of lady friends, I am not among them.' Now what was she doing? She sounded like something out of a nineteenth-century novel. She could see by the glint in Jamie's eyes that he was enjoying her discomfort.

'And what makes you so sure I have plenty of lady friends? One at a time has always been enough for me,' he replied

'Too much in some cases,' Sarah muttered under her breath to him. 'Anyway,' she said, moving towards the door, 'I really must go and see the patients in the department. You both take care of yourselves. Let me know if you need anything.'

Leaving Jamie chatting with the elderly couple, Sarah found her way back to the emergency department. Lizzie greeted her with a smile.

'How did you find Mr James? And Lucy? I heard that you and Jamie had gone up to see them.'

Sarah brought Lizzie up to date. 'I'm still a little concerned about Bill. He and his wife seem to think that everything's absolutely fine and that he'll be gone home in a few days. I just hope they're right.'

'It's up to the cardiology staff now. We've done our bit. Oh, by the way, Housekeeping brought up some theatre greens for you. It'll save your clothes from getting stained. You know where the changing rooms are.'

'Thanks, Lizzie. Is there anyone I need to see first?'

'Just the usual run-of-the-mill twisted ankles and sore throats. Dr Thompson, Keith, is stitching up a young man who had an accident with a tiling cutter and Karen is supervising the medical students at the moment. We have a couple of patients waiting for X-rays and one in the plaster room,' Lizzie said as she checked the board on which all the patients being seen were logged. 'That's it. Between us we have everything under control. The juniors know to call you or Dr Campbell if they have any concerns and before they discharge anyone home.' She looked at Sarah speculatively. 'By the way, how do you and Jamie know each other?'

It was a question Sarah had been dreading. 'We trained together,' she said evasively. Although she liked and trusted the young nurse in front of her, she wasn't ready to divulge too much of her private life. Hospitals had always been hotbeds of gossip and the last thing she wanted was for her and Jamie to become the main topic.

'He's rather gorgeous, don't you think? Half the female staff are smitten with him. I could fancy him myself if I wasn't already in love.'

Good grief, Sarah thought, exasperated, was

everyone determined to discuss Jamie with her? It was bad enough that she had to work with him without having him the subject of every conversation.

'I hadn't noticed,' Sarah lied. 'I'm not interested in men at the moment. Besides, he's not really my type. Too good-looking and impossibly conceited.'

'Conceited?' Lizzie repeated, 'I don't think I'd call him conceited. In fact, I'd say he's got very little idea of the effect he has on women.'

'I think Jamie Campbell has a very good idea of the effect he has on women,' Sarah said, a little more sharply than she'd intended. 'Now, if you'll excuse me, I'll just go and slip these on.' Leaving a bemused Lizzie in her wake, Sarah sought the relative sanctuary of the changing room.

The rest of the day was busy with a constant stream of patients requiring second opinions. She and Jamie fell into an easy working rhythm, dividing patients and the supervision of medical staff between them. When they spoke it was to discuss patients and treatment plans. It was late afternoon before Sarah managed to find time to stop for a sandwich. At least she'd have no problem losing a couple of pounds at this rate, she thought ruefully. She found a convenient vending machine and chose the least uninspiring sandwich she could find— chicken salad.

By the time she made her way back to the staffroom most of the other members of her team, including Jamie, had also taken advantage of the lull to grab a bite or a cup of coffee. Lizzie was happily filling everyone in on the details of her wedding, oblivious to the polite, resigned look on the faces around her. Clearly most, if not all, of the staff had heard it all before. She turned to Sarah, pleased to find a fresh pair of ears to regale.

'The wedding itself is going to be held in the small church in the village I grew up in a few miles out of Glasgow. I'm sorry I can't have you all there, but the church only holds around forty.' Jamie shot Sarah an amused look. She caught herself smiling back. 'The reception will be at a swish hotel on the banks of Loch

Lomond.' She named a place that Sarah knew well. It was a five-star establishment which was a favourite venue for wedding receptions amongst the well to do of the city.

'I know somebody who had their wedding there. Cost an arm and a leg,' Karen volunteered. 'I plan on settling for the registry office for mine. Whenever that might be—seeing as I haven't even met him yet!' she added with a self-deprecating chuckle.

'Well, you only get married once, and...' Lizzie looked slightly sheepish, 'I'm an only child and my father is determined to give me a wedding no one will ever forget.'

At the mention of fathers, Sarah felt a pang. She was an only child, too, but it was unlikely that her father would even be at her wedding. Not that she was ever going to get married, she reminded herself. She sneaked a look at Jamie. He was frowning, though whether at the turn the conversation was taking or at some news article in the paper he was reading that annoyed him Sarah couldn't tell.

Lizzie turned to Sarah. 'You will come to the

reception, Sarah? Everyone else is. It's on Saturday.'

'I'd love to come, Lizzie. But I'm not sure. There's Calum to think about. He'll have done without me all week. And I need to give my mum a break!'

'Can't you get a babysitter? Oh, please, come even if it's only for an hour or two,' Lizzie cajoled, determined that no one was to miss out on her big day.

'I don't know, Lizzie. I see too little of Calum as it is. I really don't like being away from him when I'm not working.'

Something in the set of Jamie's posture told Sarah he was listening in to the conversation.

'Then bring him,' Lizzie said as irrepressible as ever. 'I'm sure there will be plenty of volunteers to look after him. He's such a beautiful baby.'

Jamie stood, irritably tossing the paper to one side. 'I don't think being dragged along to a wedding is the best place for a baby.'

Sarah stared at him, dumbfounded. The rest of the staff looked uncomfortable as if this was a side to their boss they had rarely seen. 'I think it's time we all went back to work and let Dr Carruthers have her break,' Jamie continued, before leaving the room. The others, apart from Lizzie and Sarah, followed him out.

Sarah was furious. He had no right to tell her how to bring up her child. He may be the genetic father, but that didn't earn him the right to have a say in how Jamie was raised. Lizzie looked a little stricken.

'I'll see what I can do, Lizzie,' she said, 'but I can't promise anything.'

'Look, I'd love to have you there, but if it's no go then too bad.'

Sarah finished rinsing her cup before smiling at Lizzie. 'Come on, let's get back to the fray. Hopefully the patient with the suspected wrist fracture will be back from X-Ray by now.'

Sarah decided to head off at five-thirty. The department was quiet and if she left now she'd have a couple of hours to spend with Calum before bedtime. If she hurried, she just had time to pop in and see Bill on her way out. She changed out of her theatre greens and was calling out goodbye to the nursing staff when Jamie, his face sombre, called her into the duty room.

'Can't it wait, Jamie? I was just about to leave.'

Jamie looked at her, his eyes warm with sympathy.

'What is it, Jamie? What's happened?' she felt her heart begin to thud in her chest.

'I'm afraid I've got some bad news, SJ,' he said quietly.

CHAPTER FOUR

'WHAT is it? What's happened?' Sarah asked.

'I'm afraid Mr James—Bill—has taken a turn for the worse. The staff had thought he was doing well enough to have transferred him out of Intensive Care and into the cardiology ward, but he arrested shortly afterwards. They managed to resuscitate him, but I'm afraid it's only a matter of time. They have decided, with the agreement of Mary, that there is no point in taking him back to Intensive Care, and are going to make him comfortable on the ward.'

'Poor Bill—but I half expected this from the start. His age and the fact that his condition had obviously gone untreated for some time really counted against him. And poor Mary!' Sarah continued, picking up her coat. 'I was planning to go up and see them both before I went home. I'll go up now.'

'Do you have time? Aren't you in a rush to get back to Calum? I'm on call tonight. Why don't you go on home and I'll phone you if there is any change?'

Sarah felt torn. She wanted to go home. She missed her son, and missed spending time with him, even though she had only been back at work a couple of days.

'We both know that being a doctor isn't a nine-to-five job.' Sarah smiled tiredly. 'But neither is being a mother,' she continued with a rueful shake of her head. 'Now I know what these working mothers mean when they wish for a thirty-hour day.' She had always known that it would be difficult, balancing her career with being a single parent, but until today she hadn't realised just how hard it was going to be. Was she always going to feel like this? Torn between her child and her patients, even though Calum would always be her priority. Wearily she got to her feet.

'I'm going to pop up and see Mary for a few minutes at least. Maybe by the time I head off the rush-hour traffic will have eased and I'll get home at the same time anyway. And, yes, if you could ring me if there is any change—it doesn't matter what time—I'd be grateful.'

Jamie looked at her searchingly before replying. 'Of course. Would you like me to come up with you?'

'Thank you but no,' she said formally. 'I know you've got work to finish here. And anyway,' she added dryly, 'don't you have to get ready for your date?'

'Hell, I'd forgotten.' Jamie said. Sarah couldn't help a small pang of pleasure that the voluptuous Nurse Walker could be so easily dismissed from his mind. Serve the vamp right, she thought waspishly.

With a final reminder to Jamie to call her, she made her way to Cardiology where she found Mary sitting in the dim glow of the night-light, holding her husband's hand. She was talking to him in a soft voice.

'Hold on a little longer, Bill,' she was whispering. 'Jack's on his way. He won't be long. Hold on just a little while longer.'

She looked up as Sarah entered the room and managed a wan smile. 'I was just telling him to wait for Jack,' she said simply.

Sarah pulled up a chair and sat down next to the old lady. She took her free hand in hers feeling the delicate, almost papery skin under her fingers.

'Who's Jack?' she asked softly.

'Our son.' She went on in response to Sarah's look of surprise. 'Oh, yes, we have a son. He lives in the Lake District. Sadly he and his father have never hit it off. Bill was in the army and we always had to move around from place to place. We left Jack in boarding school, we thought it was for the best, but he was really unhappy and always blamed his father. It wasn't fair or right even, but I have two stubborn men. They fell out badly a couple of years ago and neither of them has been prepared to make peace. Each felt it was up to the other. Thankfully, Jack and I have always kept in touch. Occasionally I go and stay with him and his family for a few days. Bill knows and although he has always feigned disinterest,

I know he likes to hear about his son and the grandchildren. I keep in touch for both of us. I phoned Jack to let him know about his dad. He's on his way. He just wants a chance to say sorry and to tell his dad that he loves him.' Mary turned back to her sick husband. 'But you know that already, don't you, Bill?' Apart from the flutter of eyelids, there was no response from the sick man.

'I am so sorry.' Sarah said. 'I thought we had managed to save him.'

'Och, don't you worry, dear—I know it's not your fault. We both know that. It's just that Bill's time has come. If you've managed to give him a little longer—just enough to see his son and for Jack to see him one last time—we'll be forever grateful.'

Sarah swallowed the lump in her throat, at a loss for words.

The two women sat in silence for a few moments.

'Do you have anyone special in your life?' Mary asked.

'A son. Just over six months old,' Sarah replied.

'And the father?' Mary prompted gently.

'He doesn't live with us.' The dark room and the soft light made Sarah feel that she could confide in the woman looking at her with keen interest. 'He didn't—doesn't—want children,' she said, a slight break in her voice.

'Fathers are important no matter what anyone says. Every child needs a father in their life, and every father…' She hesitated, glancing at her husband's sleeping form. 'Needs his child.'

Sarah's lips twisted. Fathers needing their children? Not in her experience.

Before Sarah could formulate a suitable response, Mary looked past her to the doorway. Her faded blue eyes lit up as she saw who was standing there.

'Jack. My dearest boy, you made it!'

Jack, a man in his early forties, cast an anguished look towards the still form lying in the bed. 'Is he…?' He broke off, clearly unable to formulate the words.

'He's still alive, Jack. But he hasn't got long.'

As Jack enfolded his mother in his arms, Sarah slipped away with a few whispered words to Bill. There was no longer any reason for her to stay. The family needed their privacy now more than anything else.

As she tiptoed away pictures of her father tossing her into the air and her subsequent shrieks of laughter came trickling back. Seeing Bill and his son together after hearing about their long estrangement brought memories to the surface she had kept hidden for a long time. The hurt of his abandonment had been so profound that she had been unable to think of him in anything but the most painful way. But, she realised, it hadn't always been like that. It hadn't always been disappointment and sadness. Her father had been a charismatic man and, she was forced to admit, at least some of her memories involved laughter and fun. Perhaps if he'd been a cruel man she could have borne it better, but he hadn't been cruel, just careless of her and her feelings. Like Jamie.

Before Jamie went to check on Bill and Mary, he called into the postnatal ward to see Annie.

They had agreed that she would go over to Jamie's flat after she finished her shift at eight. That way if Jamie was called out he'd be able to go back to work at a moment's notice. But he knew it wasn't fair on Annie to let her continue to believe that there was anything more than friendship on his side. Although at the beginning the attractive midwife had said that she was only interested in a casual relationship, Jamie wondered if her feelings had changed. She had flirted outrageously with him yesterday in front of Sarah and he had to admit he had been slightly disconcerted. Annie had confided in him early on in their friendship that she had recently broken off her relationship with her boyfriend of four years.

'I just got fed up with the amount of time he was playing rugby. Every night and then at weekends. I hardly ever saw him. So I told him it was either rugby or me. And—' he could hear the hurt and indignation under the outrage '—he chose rugby.'

Jamie found Annie in the staffroom, catching up on her notes before going off duty. Not expecting to see him till their date later that evening, Annie grinned wickedly.

'Couldn't wait to see me, Dr Campbell?' she asked teasingly.

'I'm sorry to do this at the last minute, Annie, but something's come up and I can't make it tonight.'

Annie was philosophical about their broken date. 'Only one thing worse than going out with an addicted rugby player—and that's going out with a doctor.'

Jamie was taken aback. Although they had dated once or twice, he had been upfront with Annie right from the start. She knew he would be going back to Africa and wasn't up for a long-term relationship.

'I'm sorry, Annie, I think it's best that we don't see each other again, at least not romantically. I've enjoyed the time we've spent together, you're great company, but you know I'm going back to Africa soon and, besides, my life is just too complicated at the moment. Anyway I suspect, however much you try to pretend otherwise, that your heart lies elsewhere.'

Instead of appearing hurt by his words, Annie shook her head.

'Don't worry, I always knew that our relationship was never going anywhere. It's not as if you were anything less than honest about that.' She looked at him ruefully 'And you're right, if I'm honest with myself, I guess I'm still in love with Mark.' She smiled to show him there were no hard feelings. 'Actually, Mark has been on the phone several times over the last few days—I guess he heard on the hospital grapevine that I've being seeing the gorgeous Dr Campbell, and it seems that rugby doesn't have the same allure as it once had!'

Jamie looked at her suspiciously. 'Correct me if I'm wrong, but is that what yesterday's performance was about?'

Annie dropped her eyes, looking shame-faced, before her face creased into a broad smile. 'Well, it seems to have worked. You don't mind, do you?'

'Of course not. Not if it helped get you and Mark back together. But don't you think those kinds of games can be dangerous?'

'All's fair in love and war. Or so they tell me. You know if ever you need me to do the same for you, I'd be happy to oblige.'

Jamie looked into Annie's twinkling eyes. 'As I said, my life is complicated enough. I only wish *I* could be honest…' He left the sentence unfinished.

Annie looked at him searchingly. She sensed that there was a great deal that Jamie wasn't telling her, but the look in his eyes stopped her from asking. 'If ever you need a friendly ear, Jamie, you know where to find me.'

On impulse Jamie put his arm around her and squeezed her shoulders. 'Thanks, but at the moment there is nothing anyone can do to help.'

Sarah gazed lovingly at her son as he lay in his cot, his long eyelashes casting shadows on his fat pink cheeks as he drifted off to sleep for the night. Her heart felt as if it would burst with love and pride for Calum, and for the thousandth time since his birth she was glad she had made the right decision in having him. If only Jamie would allow himself to love Calum, she thought, he too could experience the wonder of their child.

Leaving the door of the bathroom open in case Calum woke up, Sarah had a quick shower. As she pulled on pyjama shorts and a camisole top, the doorbell rang. Belting up her short cotton dressing-gown, Sarah frowned as she tiptoed barefoot to the front door. Who on earth could be calling at this time of night? Keeping the chain on, she opened the door just enough to see who was standing there.

'Jamie! What are you doing here?' she asked, although from the sympathetic expression in his deep brown eyes she thought she knew.

'Can I come in for a minute? I know you said to phone, but some news is better delivered in person,' he said quietly.

Sarah unhooked the security chain and opened the door.

'It's Bill isn't it?' she stated. 'He's worse?' She felt her heart begin to thud in her chest.

'I'm so sorry, SJ, but he arrested just before ten. The ward phoned me. They did everything they could but they were unable to bring him around. He died a short while ago.'

Although Sarah had expected the news, it was still a shock. 'Oh, no!' she whispered. She was used to patients dying. She had to be, working as an A and E doctor. But Bill and his wife, and their bittersweet reunion with their estranged son, had crept under her skin. She had hoped against all odds that this was one story with a happy ending. She tried to blink away the tears blurring her vision.

Jamie stepped closer. 'Everybody did every-thing they could. You did everything you could, and gave him precious extra time to spend with his family.' Without knowing how it happened, Sarah found herself in Jamie's arms. She smelled the leather of his jacket as she rested her head against his chest.

'His poor wife, how will she cope?' she mumbled into his chest. 'They'd been married for fifty years. They were everything to each other. How does someone go on after their partner of so long leaves them?'

Jamie was a little taken aback by her reaction.

He had always known that Sarah let herself become attached to patients. But she usually hid it well, only ever showing a professional, cool exterior. Perhaps motherhood had changed her, softened her? Jamie was unprepared for the surge of protectiveness he felt as he stroked her hair tenderly. As she started to pull away, he cupped her face, gently wiping away her spilt tears with his thumbs. 'At least Mary still has her son and he'll be of some comfort and support to her.' Jamie soothed softly. 'And Bill was able to make his peace before he died.'

Remembering what Mary had said about fathers and sons, Sarah longed to blurt out the words that raged in her heart as she searched Jamie's eyes for some clue as to how he felt about her and Calum. Why couldn't he love her? And their son? Exhaustion and emotion brought fresh tears welling up in her eyes once more. 'Shh, it's OK, SJ,' Jamie said huskily, and before she knew it, he was kissing her salty, wet cheeks, tracing the tears tracks down her face and then finding her lips and tenderly covering her mouth with his own.

Sarah clung to him, breathing in his intoxicating male scent. The smell of him and the taste of his lips sent her dormant hormones into overdrive. All she could think of as Jamie's kisses became deeper, more demanding was how much she wanted him inside her. Maybe it was a reaction to Bill's death, but for the moment neither the past nor the future mattered more than her imperative need.

She slipped her hands under the front of his T-shirt, feeling the muscles of his chest bunch and tense at her touch. She let her hands travel across his skin, first finding the indent of muscle at his lower back and then, as he groaned, pulling her hips towards him, she moved her hands, as light as butterflies, to just above his jeans button to the crisp hair on his abdomen.

Jamie removed his jacket, tossing it onto the floor. In the same swift movement he removed her dressing-gown and pulled her camisole top off over her head. Her nipples tightened with desire as he cupped them gently in hands still rough from years of climbing.

Jamie could not believe he had her in his arms

again. And she had come so easily, as if they had never been apart, as if the feelings between them had not lessened with time. How soft and pliant she was, how inviting… The cold intrusive voice of reason made him falter. But was this fair to her? To revive a love affair that should stay ended? What the hell was he doing? He grabbed hold of her hips again but this time it was to peel her away from him.

'I'm sorry, SJ,' he groaned, 'I can't.'

Sarah stepped away from him as if she had been slapped. *He was rejecting her? Again? Did he think she was some sex-starved floozy who had been waiting for him to return so she could grapple him back into bed?*

Before Sarah could think of the words to persuade him that her reaction meant nothing, a loud wail tore through the air.

'What on earth is that?' Jamie asked.

'Calum,' Sarah said quietly. 'He must be looking for his next feed.'

For a moment Sarah and Jamie looked at one another. She felt slightly dazed. With trembling fingers she scooped up her camisole top and hurriedly pulled it on. Her cheeks flushed with embarrassment, Sarah tiptoed silently into the nursery, leaving the door slightly ajar so that she could attend to Calum without switching on the bedside light. As soon as she picked him up, his loud cries changed to whimpers.

Jamie appeared behind her. 'I'd better go,' he said softly.

'Yes, perhaps you should,' Sarah whispered, not trusting herself to look at him. Suddenly she remembered his date with Annie Walker. Unbidden, an image of the gorgeous midwife warming his bed sprang to her mind. Was that why he had pulled back? 'Ah, your prior arrangement with Nurse Walker—she'll be wondering where you are,' she stated flatly, anger rising, overcoming her embarrassment. What a stupid, lust-ridden, idiot he must think her.

Narrowing his eyes, Jamie said tightly, 'Actually, Sarah, I cancelled my date with Annie tonight.'

'Why?' Sarah said, turning away from him so he couldn't read the spurt of happiness she felt in her eyes. His voice was terse. 'Because, like you, I have more than enough to deal with right now without—' Before he could complete the sentence Calum began to cry in earnest.

'Here,' she said, handing him to Jamie 'You hold him while I go heat up a bottle. I don't suppose you can change a nappy?'

Jamie looked at Sarah in dismay. He was holding Calum at arm's length, as if he were some kind of foreign object. 'Change a nappy?' he echoed. 'You're not serious?'

'Why not? You'll have to learn some time. Whatever else you are, Jamie, you are this child's father, whether you like it or not.' Sarah said, and turned on her heel, leaving her son and his father alone together.

Jamie looked at the small bundle he was holding. Calum's cries had stopped and he was looking at Jamie with interest.

'Hello, there,' Jamie said.

Calum kicked his legs vigorously in response. For one horrifying moment Jamie thought he would drop the baby and changed his grip, holding him in his arms the way he had held hundreds of small children in his career. But this wasn't any child. This was *his* child. A surge of love and tenderness for his son caught Jamie unawares. Oh, God, he groaned inwardly. What sort of future had he inflicted on this innocent baby? He *had* to find out the blood results before he became any more involved with either of them. He closed his eyes against the image of life without Sarah or Calum.

'Ubh,' he said as tiny, strong fingers reached forward and gripped his lower lip, yanking it forward. His eyes shot open, to meet those of his son regarding him intently. Strong hands. Jamie thought past the pain. He'll make a good rock climber with a grip like that. And as an image of himself and his son several years older, climbing together, passed through his mind, Jamie realised that for the second time in his life he had fallen hopelessly and irrevo- cably in love.

Heated bottle in hand, Sarah stood watching Jamie and her son. *Their* son. He seemed so relaxed with his child and Calum in his turn seemed happy and contented with his father. She felt confused. What did it all mean? Jamie taking her in his arms, playing with his child. And how did she feel about it? She needed to know what was going on inside Jamie's head.

'Let me change Calum's nappy and give him his feed. Then perhaps we can talk once he's asleep,' she suggested.

Jamie stood up, handing the baby over.

'Talk about what, Sarah?' he asked softly

'Us. You and me. Well, maybe not us.' She stumbled over the words. That wasn't what she'd intended to say. He obviously had no intention of there being an 'us'. 'You and Calum.'

'Of course I'll make sure you are both well provided for financially.'

'Financially?' Sarah echoed, feeling the blood in her veins turn to ice. 'Is that what you think I want? Financial help with a bit of sex on the side?'

'I'm sorry if I gave you the wrong impression, but I don't think I can give you an answer to what you're asking—not yet.'

Sarah felt her cheeks burn with embarrassment. She had got it wrong—again! For a blind moment she had allowed herself to believe that

Jamie wanted her as much as she wanted him. But what was even worse, he didn't seem to want Calum either!

'You can't keep popping in and out of our lives, Jamie. Calum, at least, has a right to either have you in his life with all the commitment that entails or you have to stay out of our lives. For his sake—and mine.' She lifted her chin, determined not to let him know how much her words were costing her. She couldn't—wouldn't—let him see how much she was hurting.

'I need some time SJ. That's all I'm asking. At the moment I can't give either of you what you are looking for.'

'Then I think you'd better leave, don't you?'

Jamie went over to the sofa and retrieved his jacket. 'Of course. I shouldn't have come.' He looked at Sarah and then at his son. Sarah could see something close to anguish reflected in his eyes. 'Goodbye, SJ,' he said softly as he gently closed the door behind him.

CHAPTER FIVE

SARAH crept into the department, praying that she'd be able to avoid Jamie until she had some strong coffee under her belt. What had she been thinking? Falling into his arms like some overwrought child? But she knew her response to Jamie had been anything but that of a child. She almost groaned aloud as she remembered how his body had felt, hard and muscular against hers. She felt her cheeks go pink as she thought of his lips trailing across her shoulders, finding the secret spot at the base of her throat that he knew from past experience drove her wild. Stupid, stupid, stupid, she berated herself. How could she have succumbed so quickly to his touch, thought for one moment that his feelings had changed? That he was ready to make a commitment, if not to her, at least to their son.

Nothing more. She felt her blush deepen as she remembered the scene, how easily she had gone into his arms. He wasn't even interested in sex. He had rejected her. She would have gone to bed with him and he knew it. Was the thought of being with her so repulsive to him? Did he think that once they had slept together she would make demands on him? Demands that he clearly didn't want. He had made that perfectly clear.

With a sinking heart she realised she was going to have to find a way to keep him at arm's length. Clearly she couldn't trust the responses of her own traitorous body. Could she persuade him to go back to Africa early? If financial support was all he was prepared to offer, she and Calum would be better off without him. Surely the department could find someone else, even at short notice? But the mere thought of Jamie being thousands of miles away sent her spirits plummeting. She didn't know which would be worse—seeing him every day, yet not being able to have him in the only sense she truly wanted him, completely and wholly hers, or never seeing him at all. Damn him. Why did he have to come back and upset her neatly ordered life? Just when she'd thought she'd got over him.

As she stepped into the department, Lizzie thrust a cup of hot black coffee into her hand.

'Thank you. You must be psychic,' said Sarah. 'How did you know it was the one thing I truly needed right at this moment?'

'I'm getting to know you. You run better when you're kept well fuelled. Besides, we have a young man with multiple injuries coming in in a few minutes. He was found at the bottom of the Clyde Bridge. No one knows what happened. Whether he fell, jumped or was pushed. Looks like we're going to need all hands on deck. So drink up. It might be your last chance for a while.'

Sarah took a couple of sips of her coffee before setting it down and going to change into her theatre greens. Mentally she ran through the possible injuries that she might be faced with in the next few minutes. As she emerged from the changing room, she noticed that Karen was in some sort of heated discussion with a patient.

Judging by the expression on her face, Karen's usual good humour seemed to have deserted her, and Sarah thought she knew why.

'Just give me a prescription for the pain, and I'll be on my way,' the patient shouted at Karen.

Sarah went over to them, noticing that the man was scruffily dressed and wore a woollen hat pulled low over his brow.

'Can I help?' she asked politely.

'The doctor here won't give me a prescription for my pain!' the man said angrily

'I'm sure if Dr Davidson here doesn't feel you need a prescription then she is absolutely right, Mr…?'

'Wilson. Kenny Wilson,' The man replied truculently.

'This is the second time Mr Wilson has been here in as many weeks.' Karen said, unmistakably exasperated. 'I've explained that we don't give out strong painkillers for headaches, but he's not happy with my decision.'

'I assume he's been thoroughly examined?'

'Of course. There is absolutely nothing to be found. I've checked with one or two of the other A and E departments and he's a regular attender there, too.' She shot Sarah a significant look. Sarah knew what it meant. Every department had their share of drug-addicted patients. While Sarah sympathised with anyone whose life had hit rock bottom, an A and E department was not the place to get the help they needed.

Kenny took a step towards Sarah, so close she could smell the alcohol on his breath. It took all her nerve not to step back. 'You doctors are all the same,' he hissed.

'I think it's time you left,' a low voice said from behind Sarah. 'Now, are you going to leave quietly or shall I get Security to escort you off the premises?'

Kenny took one look at Jamie's muscular frame and uncompromising expression before deciding that discretion was the better part of valour. He sidled towards the exit, grumbling volubly.

'Thanks, Sarah, Jamie,' said Karen. 'I must admit I was relieved you came along when you did. But now, if you'll excuse me, I have a couple of patients waiting to see me.' As she left them, Jamie looked at Sarah. 'Are you all right?'

'I'm perfectly fine,' she said. It was her turn to be annoyed. 'I know you meant well, Jamie, but when are you going to realise I'm a big girl now and perfectly able to take care of myself and my staff?'

'I've never been in any doubt that you can. You made that crystal clear again last night.'

'Please, forget about last night, Jamie. I should never have…' She searched for the right words. 'Kissed you,' she managed at last, although they both knew it had been much more than that. She would have gone to bed with him, if Jamie hadn't pulled away. She suspected he knew that and cringed inwardly. 'It's just that you caught me at a vulnerable moment.' Sarah said stiffly, her cheeks flushing at the memory.

'It was my fault,' Jamie answered. 'But I'm not sure I want to forget about it entirely.' He smiled lazily.

'Well, it's not going to happen again!' Sarah retorted. 'So can we, please, just stick to talking about work?'

'Sarah I…' Jamie started. 'No, you're right.

It's best if we stick to clinical subjects for the time being.' Before Sarah could think about his words he went on, 'You've heard we're expecting a young man with multiple trauma?' He paused as the wail of an ambulance got louder and then shut off abruptly. 'Sounds like he's just arrived. Come on. Let's go.'

While the patient was being wheeled into Resus, the paramedics reeled off information on his status.

'Twenty-four-year-old, name's Tom Kennedy, according to his driving licence. Discovered unconscious at the foot of the Clyde Bridge half an hour ago by a member of the public. Has a GCS of 6, BP 90 over 45, pulse 125 and respirations 18 per minute. Bleeding extensively from a head wound, fractured right tibia and fibula, which have been stabilised. Bruising to abdomen.' The room filled up with medical and nursing staff as they all gathered around the gurney where the patient lay.

'OK,' Sarah said, snapping on gloves. 'Is someone stabilising his head and neck? Good. On my count of three remove the stretcher underneath him.' Once the manoeuvre was completed with practised timing, Lizzie gently and expertly cut away the bloodied clothes from Tom.

The paramedic continued, 'No morphine given due to his poor level of consciousness and respiratory distress. IV fluids given stat and second litre of saline almost through. Twenty-eight per cent Oxygen running at 6 litres via a trauma mask.'

Before Jamie put on the gown and gloves that one of the nursing staff held out for him he passed Sarah a pair of protective goggles. Sarah glanced around the room to ensure that all the staff were wearing theirs.

'I'll take care of his airway and head injury if that's OK with you, Sarah?' Jamie suggested, already preparing to insert an endotracheal tube into the man's airway.

'Fine. Keith and I will check out the rest of his injuries.' Looking up briefly, Sarah turned to Elspeth, one of the older nurses who had worked in the department for years. 'Call Theatre and let them know we might need them. Lizzie, can you—?'

But Lizzie had already anticipated her request

and was moving towards the telephone. 'Call X-Ray and arrange a head CT scan, chest and abdo x-rays, and page Orthopaedics—already on it!'

Dr Thompson placed the leads from the cardiac monitor onto Tom's chest. As the Dinamap—the machine that measured blood pressure, oxygen saturation and pulse rate—alarmed, he called out, 'BP dropping—80 over 40, pulse 130.'

'OK.' Sarah remained calm, her fingers deftly examining the abdomen and chest of the patient lying motionless in front of her. 'Let's get some more fluids into him while we're waiting for blood to be cross-matched. A bag of Hartmann's stat, please, Lizzie.' Frowning slightly, Sarah placed her stethoscope on the left side of Tom's chest.

'Need a hand?' Jamie asked, his eyes intent through his protective visor. 'He's intubated, airway patent and clear. His pupils are responding to light but nothing further to be done regarding his head injury until we get that scan.'

Sarah nodded at Jamie. 'He's got a left-sided tension pneumothorax—he needs a chest drain

now! Elspeth, can you pass me a kit, please?'
Lizzie and Elspeth exchanged worried looks.
They knew how serious this condition could
be, and there could be other hidden injuries,
too.

Swabbing the area over his left side with
antiseptic to sterilise the skin, Sarah took the
scalpel from Jamie with steady hands. Before
she could make contact with the skin, however,
the heart monitor emitted a warning bell.

'He's in AF!' Keith called out urgently.

'Carry on, Sarah, we'll keep ventilating him,'
Jamie calmly responded, attaching an ambu-
bag to the tube he had inserted earlier.

Too focused on her patient to be aware of the
mounting tension in the room, she made the
small incision into the intercostal space without
hesitation. Glancing up she caught Jamie's
almost imperceptible nod of encouragement,
both knowing how one wrong slip could be
catastrophic. But there was no time to waste.
They had to get the young man's circulation
going again and the insertion of the drain was
crucial. Taking a long, thin plastic tube, she

pushed it with an equal amount of strength and gentleness between Tom's ribs and into his chest. Suddenly the tube filled with frothy red blood, pouring into the container that it was securely attached to on the floor. Immediately the heart monitor stopped its shrill warning and was replaced by the reassuring beeps that indicate a steady heart rhythm.

'Right, folks, he's stable. Let's get him to Radiology for a CT scan to determine the extent of his head injury.' As Sarah and Jamie rushed the gurney through the bay, Lizzie cleared their path, pushing the resus equipment trolley to one side and sweeping away the discarded debris of dressing packs and empty syringes scattered on the floor with her foot. They were just outside the swing doors of the X-ray department when they were intercepted by one of the triage staff nurses. 'Mrs Kennedy, the patient's mother, has arrived. Can one of you speak to her?' she asked.

'Off you go, Sarah. Keith and I will stay with Tom,' Jamie offered.

'Thanks. Staff Nurse, I'll be along in a

minute. In the meantime, can you put Mrs Kennedy in the relatives' room, please?'

Sarah peeled off her gloves and removed her blood-splattered theatre gown, using the brief respite to compose herself. Breaking bad news to relatives was one aspect of her job she found extremely difficult, but at least this time she was confident Tom would survive his injuries. There was every chance he would make a full recovery, although there would be an anxious few hours ahead for all of them. Once Tom had recovered sufficiently, the police would wish to interview him. She wondered what tragic set of circumstances had led to Tom's broken body being found at the foot of the bridge.

After leaving a tearful but grateful Mrs Kennedy a short time later, Sarah went to join Jamie in X-Ray. She found him in discussion with the radiologist, both studying the images displayed on the computer screen.

'What's the verdict?' she asked, peering over Jamie's shoulder.

He glanced back at her, a smile dimpling his cheek. 'Good news—no fracture or evidence of brain swelling. In fact, he's just beginning to regain consciousness. This is one lucky young man, wouldn't you say, SJ?'

'Thank goodness for that,' she said. 'He'll be going to Theatre for the orthopods to set his leg, then hopefully High Dependency will have a bed for him.' Suddenly the adrenaline of the past hour drained away and Sarah felt exhausted, and guessed that Jamie would be feeling the same way. Whatever her personal feelings, they were still professional colleagues who depended on one another. 'Fancy a coffee?' she offered. 'I'll make it this time, after I update his mother.'

'Great. Give me ten while I brief the surgeons on Tom, and I'll meet you in the staffroom.'

Sarah slumped in the saggy chair in the staffroom. She yawned. What she wouldn't do for one completely uninterrupted night's sleep. Lizzie came in and plonked herself down in the chair next to Sarah's with a heavy sigh. Her normally cheerful face was drawn and a frown puckered her brow.

'What it is Lizzie?' Sarah asked, concerned. 'Everything going all right for the wedding? With you and Stewart?'

'Oh, the wedding!' She shook her head dismissively. 'No, the arrangements are going fine. Can't wait for the honeymoon. Chance to put my feet up and get a long rest.' Sarah shot her a mischievous look that brought spots of colour to Lizzie's pale cheeks. 'OK I'm looking forward to the honeymoon for other reasons, too. Stewart and I have hardly spent any time alone in the last month. There always seems to be somebody there, talking about arrangements. I'm beginning to wonder if there is life outside work and the wedding. And I thought I'd never get tired of planning my big day!' She laughed, but then looked serious again. 'No there's something else. A work-related matter I need to discuss with you. And I'm afraid you're not going to be happy when you hear what I have to say.'

'OK. But let me get you a coffee first.' Once the two women had got settled, Lizzie started in a hesitant voice.

'Morphine has gone missing from the resus trolley.'

'Are you sure?' Sarah asked. 'When so many doctors and nurses are dipping into the trolley during an emergency, isn't it hard to keep track of what's been used?'

'That's just it,' Lizzie continued unhappily. 'It's part of my job to ensure that everything is accounted for and written up correctly. After an emergency, I immediately recheck the trolley and reorder everything that has been removed. But today there was an ampoule of morphine missing—and Tom wasn't given any morphine. I checked first with all the medical staff as perhaps in the commotion it was taken for another patient by one of them, but so far no one is admitting to it. Anyway, at the very least there should be an empty ampoule. I looked everywhere for it—I even tried to empty the sharps bin.'

'That's a bit risky surely? You could get a needle-stick injury.'

Lizzie dismissed Sarah's reproachful tone with a wave of her fingers.

'I took the appropriate precautions. And what's more, this is the second time in two weeks that it's happened. I didn't mention the first incident to anyone but my nurse manager, as I was sure that it was a one-off incident. That someone had simply forgotten to write it up.'

'But now you think differently?' Sarah prompted

'For sure. Once is unlikely, but possible. Twice…' She shook her head. 'And it gets worse.'

Sarah waited for Lizzie to continue. She was obviously choosing her words with care.

'Someone saw Jamie, Dr Campbell, slip a couple of syringes and needles into his pocket the other evening.'

Sarah almost laughed aloud. Surely Lizzie couldn't be suggesting that Jamie had anything to do with the missing drugs?

Lizzie caught Sarah's expression. 'Of course it's ludicrous thinking that Jamie would take the morphine, but if we knew why he took the other stuff, at least we could rule him out.' Lizzie looked at Sarah imploringly. 'I should really go straight to my boss about this, but if there is any chance that you and I could get to the bottom of it first, I'll wait until tomorrow.' She stood up.

'However, if we still don't have an answer as to what happened to the drugs, I'll have no choice but to formally report it.'

'I'm sure that there is a perfectly innocent reason for Jamie's action and I'm confident the mystery of the syringes will be easily cleared up. Perhaps he was going up to one of the wards to take blood from a patient there?'

'Possible, but unlikely. He was off duty, Sarah. On his way home,' Lizzie said miserably. 'And you and I both know that consultants rarely take blood. That's usually left to the junior doctors. Besides, the wards have their own supplies of needles and syringes.'

'There still could be a hundred different innocent reasons why Jamie took the syringes as I'm sure we'll find out when I ask him. In the meantime, do you have any idea who else might be desperate enough to risk their career by stealing controlled drugs?'

'I know my nurses pretty well. Most of them

have worked here for years. I just can't believe that any of them would do anything so stupid. One or two of them do have personal problems—as you'd expect to find in any large department. Elspeth, for example has a mother with chronic arthritis who suffers with severe pain. But as I said, she's worked with me for years and I can't see her doing anything so dim-witted, not to mention illegal!'

'What about other staff—porters, clerical staff, plaster-room technicians?'

'I suppose it's always possible. But they aren't usually in Resus. In fact, apart from the odd radiologist, there really is only us doctors and nurses.'

'But there *could* be others. Look, Jamie will be along in a minute and I'll talk to him about it. Ask if he has any ideas.' Sarah reflected for a moment. She hated the thought that any of her staff could be under suspicion—even for a moment.

'Actually, Lizzie, there was a patient in here this morning. Karen saw him. Apparently he had been trying to get her to prescribe him some strong painkillers and she refused. Why don't you track her down and find out when he came in and when he was last here? If she doesn't know, the triage nurses would have made a note of dates and times on his attendance card.'

'I don't see how that will help us *prove* anything,' Lizzie said a little doubtfully.

'At least it will show that someone else apart from staff could be involved. Don't worry, Lizzie,' Sarah said softly, 'one way or another we'll get to the bottom of this.'

'I hope we do,' replied an unconvinced Lizzie, 'I couldn't bear to have this hanging over us all at the wedding.'

Once the nurse had left the room, Sarah sat deep in thought. This was one side of her new role that she would never like. Acting as a policeman, looking at her colleagues, her hard-working and dedicated colleagues, with suspicion was anathema to her. The sooner they got this cleared up the better for the whole department. She jumped when the duty-room door flew open.

'Where's that coffee, then?' Jamie teased, striding into the room.

As Sarah handed him a cup, she paused awkwardly. 'There's something I need to discuss with you.'

Jamie made himself comfortable, stretching his long legs in front of him and putting his arms behind his head before narrowing his eyes at her.

'It's not anything to do with Calum—or last night. I told you I want us to stick to talking about work—and I meant it.' she said through gritted teeth, noting his wary look. 'No, this is something else entirely.'

Jamie visibly relaxed and leaned back in the chair. The movement caused the top of his hospital greens to ride up. Catching a glimpse of tanned muscle, Sarah's couldn't stop her thoughts flying back to the night before. With an effort she forced herself to concentrate on the issue at hand.

'Apparently someone has removed controlled drugs from the resus trolley on two occasions. Two weeks ago and today. And,' she went on baldly 'you were seen slipping some syringes and needles into your pocket the other evening.'

Jamie stared at Sarah, at first with disbelief

and then, when he realised she was serious, with deepening anger.

'And you have linked the two events. I was seen taking syringes, *ergo* I must also be a drug addict—or, worse, a drug dealer who has so little regard for his patients or his career that he plunders drugs from the hospital he's working in.'

'Of course I don't suspect you. I can't imagine anyone less likely to be stealing drugs. And once you tell me why you took the syringes, you can help me find out who did really take the drugs.' She looked at Jamie expectantly.

Jamie shook his head. 'I'm afraid I can't tell you why I took the syringes. You are just going to have to trust me that it was not for the purpose of administering drugs, either to myself or anyone else.'

'I'm afraid that's not good enough, Jamie.' Sarah stiffened her resolve in the face of Jamie's anger. Of course she had the right to question him. And he knew it. 'I need to know for sure that you had nothing to do with the missing drugs.'

Jamie glared at her, incredulity written all over his face.

'I can't believe you are even asking the question. Good God, woman, don't you know me better than that?'

'But I don't really know you at all, do I? I thought I did, once. But now I realise I don't know you at all.'

Jamie frowned. 'I didn't take those drugs, Sarah.' He stood up. 'And as far as I'm concerned, that is all you need to know. But may I suggest if you really want to find your thief, you take a look at the CCTV footage from the last couple of days. If you still have no joy, then I suggest you call in the police.' And with one final glare, he turned on his heel and stalked out of the room.

Well! thought Sarah furiously. *Just who did he think he was?* Of course she didn't really believe, not for one moment, that he had taken the drugs, but on the other hand his refusal to tell her why he had taken the needles and syringes, his behaviour over the last few days—there was *something* he wasn't telling her.

Nevertheless, she would do as he'd suggested. Look at what the CCTV cameras had recorded over the last few days. In fact, the more she thought about it, the more she was certain that the only time the trolley had been unlocked had been earlier that day, when the man with the terrible injuries had been treated. It was possible that Kenny had slipped back when their attention had been on Tom. With a bit of luck, something would show up on the security camera.

On her way to see the head of security, Sarah bumped into a harassed-looking Lizzie.

'I've managed to pull Kenny Wilson's records up on the computer. He was in the department on both dates. However, he was signed out of the department shortly after Tom was admitted.'

'I think it's possible that he might have sneaked back in while we were all occupied with Tom. Jamie suggested looking at CCTV footage to see whether there is anything on camera that will help, so I'm just heading off to find the security manager now.'

'Did you ask Jamie about the syringes?'

'Yes, I did, and I have to say I didn't handle it very well.'

'What did he say?'

'Only that he didn't take the drugs, which I knew, and that I should check with Security. Honestly, Lizzie, I do love my job, the medical side at least, but I don't think I realised exactly what I was getting in for when I took the head of department role.'

Lizzie smiled in sympathy. 'Hey, you're doing a great job. Staff morale has never been higher. We all know how hard you work. Jamie, too. I just worry sometimes you try to do too much.'

'It comes with the territory, but thanks for the vote of confidence. On days like today I can do with all the encouragement I can get.'

Soon Sarah was sitting down with the head of hospital security, a middle-aged man called George, reviewing the tapes. She had had to tell him why she needed to see the footage. It had taken all Sarah's powers of persuasion, but eventually George had reluctantly agreed to spend a few minutes going over the tapes before they involved management and the police.

'You should have come straight to me. Sister York should have come to me after the first incidence. That's what we are here for,' he had grumbled.

'I know, but I'm here now. And if we can get this sorted out without any of the staff feeling that they are under suspicion, then that can only be a good thing, surely?' Sarah had said placatingly.

'You could have trusted me to handle the matter discreetly. I agree with you, though. There's no point in getting staff all hot and bothered before we have to.'

'I'm sorry, George. Next time—God forbid there is a next time—I'll come to you immediately. I promise.'

While they had been talking, George had found and loaded the tapes from the period when Kenny had been in the department up to and including the time when Tom had been in Resus.

She could see blurred images of herself, Jamie and the other medical and nursing staff moving in and out of the picture.

George stopped the tape.

'There. Do you see?'

At first all Sarah could see was the figures of the five or six staff who were working over the trolley on which Tom lay. The security officer pressed a button and the picture panned out, revealing more of the resus room. The emergency trolley had been pushed out of everyone's way and rested near the open door of the room. As the officer showed Sarah the pictures frame by frame, a figure appeared from the door and a hand casually dipped into the trolley and removed a vial. The picture was too grainy for her to make out the contents, but she had a pretty good idea what it was. George manipulated the computer and the face of the figure came into view. Sarah recognised him at once. It was Kenny Wilson. Just as she'd suspected. Then George ran the tapes from the date Lizzie had given her when Kenny had attended previously. It took twenty minutes but eventually they found what they'd been looking for. It was a similar scenario to the one that day. This time two patients with severe injuries had been treated simultaneously and most of the department's medical and nursing staff had been occupied in trying to save their lives. From the footage Sarah could see that Kenny had hung around the department for a considerable time before choosing his moment to remove something from the trolley. He had taken a terrible risk, but had almost got away with it. Sarah felt enormous relief. At least it wasn't a member of staff. But clearly they would have to do something about security. Warn other hospitals in the city. She made a mental note to add it to her management agenda.

As if reading her thoughts, George said, 'Your security isn't up to much, is it? I think I should come around tomorrow and spend the day in the department, reviewing your procedures.'

Sarah sighed. Just one more task to get in the way of her seeing patients. Still, it was a small price to pay for peace of mind. She stood up, thanking George warmly for his help. She needed to find Lizzie and Jamie as soon as she could. At least she knew for certain that Jamie hadn't taken the missing drugs. But why had he taken the syringes? Why didn't he trust her? *And didn't she trust him?* The small niggling voice was back. *With her life, yes. But not her heart, not ever again*

Sarah found Lizzie suturing a patient who had sliced open a finger with a kitchen knife. She waited until the nurse had finished and had sent the patient on her way with instructions to see her GP in seven days to have the stitches removed. Once the treatment room was empty of patients, Sarah filled Lizzie in on what she had found out.

Lizzie gave a sigh of relief, the worry clearing from her eyes. 'Thank goodness. I was going mad, thinking that it might be a colleague stealing drugs.' She frowned again as she remembered her concerns about Jamie. 'Have you told Jamie?'

'Not yet. I will as soon as I catch him on his own. I'm sure he'll be pleased we've found the real culprit. He was furious when he thought I was suspecting him of taking the drugs.'

'To be fair, it wasn't an altogether unreasonable assumption. After all, how well do any of us know him? He's only been here a couple of weeks and although I have nothing but admiration for his clinical skills, we know very little about his personal life. He never talks about himself. But, still, I should have known that he is too fine a doctor to even have been a possibility. It would never have crossed my mind if it hadn't been for the syringes.'

She looked at Sarah who had suddenly busied herself putting away swabs. 'Oh, I'd forgotten. You knew him before, didn't you?'

Sarah thought rapidly. How much should she reveal about her true relationship with Jamie? It was likely that she and Lizzie would be working closely for years to come. But, on the other hand, if she told her, could Lizzie resist telling the others? It wasn't as if Jamie was going to be around for very much longer. She looked at the nurse and met her frank gaze. Somehow she knew instinctively that she could trust Lizzie with her secret.

'Can I trust you to keep something to yourself? I need to know that what I'm about to tell you will go no further.'

'You have my word.' Lizzie grinned. 'Cross my heart and hope to die.' She made the gesture with her fingers. Then the smile left her face. 'You know, Sarah, working in emergency medicine, you get used to hearing and keeping secrets. I promise anything you tell me will go with me to the grave.'

Sarah returned Lizzie's candid look for a few moments before continuing.

'Jamie and I first met while we were both at medical school. We didn't hang out with the same crowd. He and his pals were considered the wild ones. Partying every night and climbing every weekend. My friends were the more studious, quieter set. But somehow,' Sarah recalled smiling, 'he still managed to get the best marks. He did ask me out once, but he had a reputation for being a bit of a womaniser so I said no. Then we met again as registrars. He still seemed a little wild, but instead of directing his energy into parties and womanising, he was putting it into extreme sports when he wasn't working every hour he could. The consultants and the patients loved him. He asked me out again and although I turned him down several times, he persisted until finally I gave in and agreed to go out with him.' Sarah paused.

'We discovered a shared passion for hill

walking and he introduced me to climbing. We were inseparable until…'

'Go on.' Lizzie encouraged.

'Until we had finished our training and were eligible for consultant jobs. One day, almost out of the blue, he told me that he was going to Africa to work for a couple of years.'

'Didn't he ask you to go, too?'

'No. From the beginning he made it clear that he wasn't prepared to commit himself to anyone. Would never get married. In fact, I think it was when I raised the possibility of a future and children that he made his decision to go.' She couldn't stop the bitterness seeping into her voice.

'And you thought that you could change him. That you'd be the one that would make him want to commit?'

Sarah smiled wryly. 'I suppose so. It makes me sound a little naïve. He never gave me a reason to think he had changed his mind except…' Sarah's voice cracked a little. 'Except I really thought he loved me. In fact, until he told me he was leaving, I never doubted it for a moment.'

'Sounds like he really hurt you. That he was a bit of a lad on the women front,' Lizzie said sympathetically. 'To be honest, the gossip around here is that he has someone back in Africa. Elspeth overheard him talking on the phone the other day, he seemed to be promising someone that he'd be back soon. And then there's Annie Walker from upstairs.'

Sarah smiled bitterly. 'He does seem to have his hands full and I guess with hindsight it's obvious the suggestion of commitment was enough to make him run a mile. All I know is that I was desperately in love with him. I believed I had found the person I was going to spend the rest of my life with. And I was so sure he felt the same way. How wrong I was.'

'And you never heard from him after he left?'

'Not a word.' It was all Sarah could do to disguise the pain she still felt at his sudden abandonment of her.

'He must have been surprised to find out you had a son.' Lizzie caught the expression on Sarah's face and Sarah could see from her widened eyes that the whole truth was beginning to dawn.

'How long is it since you last saw him?'

'Fifteen months ago,' Sarah admitted reluctantly.

'Calum's his son, isn't he? I thought there was something familiar about your son. But I never guessed.' Lizzie looked dumbfounded. 'Does Jamie know? About Calum? Of course he must know. You'll have told him when you found out you were pregnant.'

Sarah hesitated, thinking back to the day she had taken the pregnancy test. 'I didn't tell him. I decided there was no point. He only found out the day I started work here. He had no idea I had had his child and I had no idea he worked here. So it was a bit of a shock for both of us.'

'And now? Surely, now he knows about Calum, he wants to be part of your lives?'

'Not noticeably. He came around to my flat last night and met Calum properly for the first time. Although he seemed taken with him, he told me he's not ready to make anything but a financial commitment to Calum. As if I need or want his money! Neither do I want someone in Calum's life who is only there when it suits him. Heaven knows, I had enough of that sort of father to realize it's not what I want for my child. Calum deserves a father who is going to be around. Someone who will always be there for him. Not someone who lives halfway across the world and who puts his own needs first.'

'Funny, I would never have thought of him as a man who would abandon his child. But, then, as I said, I don't really know him.'

'I was convinced I knew him. But obviously I don't at all. I suppose there are plenty of men just like him, who run a mile from responsibility. But I'm sorry, I shouldn't have told you so much.' Sarah leaned over and placed a hand on Lizzie's arm. 'Please, don't share this information with anyone else, Lizzie. I couldn't bear it if my personal life became common knowledge. What's more, whatever one can say about Jamie Campbell as a man, he really is one hell of a doctor. And as far as this department is concerned, that's all that matters.'

CHAPTER SIX

KEITH THOMPSON waylaid Sarah as she left Lizzie in the treatment room.

'Do you have a moment, Dr Carruthers?' No matter how often Sarah had tried to tell him to call her by her first name, he insisted on using her full title. It amused her to think that Keith held her in the same awe that she had held her consultants as a junior. She didn't feel that old—or that wise.

'Sure. Is there a problem?'

'I have an elderly lady with cardiac pain who needs to be admitted. The trouble is she's refusing. She's the sole carer of her forty-year-old son who has Down's syndrome. Says he can't be left on his own. He came in the ambulance with her. She won't let me call Social Services either. When I suggested it she became quite agitated. In fact, she's getting dressed to leave and I don't know how to stop her.'

'Would you like me to have a word with her?' Sarah asked.

'Could you?' Keith sighed his relief. 'It's just if she goes home tonight without further tests and treatment, there's no telling what could happen. And it's not as if we could rely on the son to call us if there's a problem. It simply wouldn't be fair on either of them.'

'Which cubicle is she in?'

When Keith introduced her to the patient, a bright-eyed woman in her late seventies, Sarah knew she had a fight on her hands. Mrs Loveday was clearly frightened and upset, but more than that she had the air of a woman who was used to doing battle and getting her own way. Her son sat by her bedside, holding her hand. He had the distinctive features of someone with Down's. He smiled engagingly at Sarah.

'You really need to stay in overnight, Mrs Loveday,' Sarah said gently.

'Can't I come back tomorrow during the day and have the tests then? I really don't see why an overnight stay is necessary. I'd only be using up a bed. There's bound to be people who need it more than I do.'

Sarah hid a smile. Mrs Loveday reminded her of her grandmother. Another feisty soul.

'You need to stay in so we can keep you under observation overnight,' Sarah said carefully. She needed to impress the seriousness of her condition without alarming her even more. 'I know you're worried about your son—David, isn't it? But Social Services will find someone who can stay with him in your home. It will just be for a night or two.'

'If I let Social Services get their hooks into us, they'll never leave us in peace. It'll be meals on wheels, day-care centres and goodness knows what else before we know it. They'll say I'm not fit to look after David and try and take him away from me. The same as they did when he was born. Said he'd never amount to anything—that he was unlikely to talk or dress himself or go to the toilet even. Told me I should put him into care and forget about him. You see…' she grabbed Sarah's hand in a surprisingly strong grip '…I was a single mother, and in those days it was still frowned on. They said being a single mother was hard enough, without trying to bring up a handicapped child on my own.'

Her words brought memories of her own pregnancy flooding back to Sarah.

'Is that what's worrying you? You think they might take David from you permanently? I can see why you're worried, but times have changed a lot in recent years. Social Services are there to help you and David to stay together in your own home. They know that's where he belongs—with his mother.'

Mrs Loveday still didn't look convinced.

'They thought they knew better when he was born, but they were wrong. David manages to do everything by himself. Can't you, sweetheart? He can even drive a car. And he has a job.' David grinned his pleasure at his mother's praise. Then she turned to Sarah again. 'You medical people were wrong before so why should I trust you now?'

Sarah sat down on the bed next to the elderly

woman. 'You're absolutely right. We doctors have, and still can, make mistakes. We try our best not to, but at the end of the day we are only human. And when we're wrong and things turn out better for the patient than we'd predicted, we are delighted. The doctors were wrong about David. You were right to fight to keep him. All we could do then was give you an opinion based on the knowledge available at the time, but nowadays we're more clued up and are more conscientious about giving patients as much information as possible so they can make their own decisions.' Sarah thought for a moment. She could see that Mrs Loveday was beginning to waver, but she needed her to be absolutely convinced that she could trust Sarah.

'I have a little boy. He's coming up for seven months now and is a lively wee thing. But there was a time when I was pregnant that I thought he might have Down's syndrome.' Sarah noticed that she had Mrs Loveday's full attention. She stopped pulling on her clothes and sat back down, looking at Sarah with interest.

'They didn't have the tests when you were pregnant but now they do a blood test on all pregnant women that can show them if they are at increased risk of having a child with Down's. Well, my test came back indicating that there was an increased risk. I had to make a decision. I could do two things. Do nothing and wait and see. Have an amniocentesis test, which carried a small risk of miscarriage, and, following that result, decide whether or not to continue the pregnancy. After a lot of thought and after speaking to women like yourself who have Down's syndrome children, I realised what a great deal of pleasure they got from their children, and how most of them grow up, like David, into loving, reasonably independent adults. I decided to take the chance. I had almost decided once before to end the pregnancy because, like you, I was a single mother, but once I decided to go through with the pregnancy, it was as if—I don't know—I had made a commitment to my unborn baby that I would love and cherish it regardless. As they say in the marriage vows. In sickness and in health.'

Sarah paused for a moment and Mrs Loveday patted her hand in sympathy.

'So I know how scared you are. I know that you want to protect your son, but isn't it better that he gets to know and love and trust other people and places for that time, hopefully a long time from now, when you won't be around?'

'I know you're right, dear. It's just difficult to let them have their independence. You won't know about that now, but just you wait until your son grows up!'

'That time will come for me, too. As it must for all parents eventually. Take a leap of faith and accept the help Social Services can give you now. After all, if you don't look after your health, you might not be around as long as you could be. Let us look after you now and hopefully you will be there for David for many more years.'

'Very well, dear. I guess I don't really have a choice. But only if they'll send someone over to stay in the house. I don't want him upset more than he has to be.'

'I'll make sure of it,' Sarah promised. 'In the meantime, let's get you back into your gown.'

* * *

Jamie moved away from the curtain of the cubicle. He had stopped to listen when he'd caught Sarah's words about her pregnancy. He was dismayed. He had no idea that Sarah had had to face so many fears during her pregnancy on her own. He should have been there for her. And now there was a good chance he was about to inflict further months, if not years, of worry and anxiety. He had to find out if he carried the gene, and soon. He would call Robert and let him know that he had to have the result. Stat.

Jamie put the phone down with a frown. He checked in with the hospital back in Africa whenever he could and was usually reassured that they seemed to be coping without him. However, today the conversation he'd had with his colleague had worried him. Greg's usual ebullience seemed to have deserted him and his normally upbeat manner had been subdued. At first he had denied there was anything worrying him until, at Jamie's insistence, he had admitted his concerns.

'One of the more experienced doctors has

had to return to Europe unexpectedly—a family emergency,' Greg had told Jamie. 'We were coping, just about, without you, but now being two doctors down is putting a strain on our already overstretched resources. I simply can't expect anyone to do more. We're all working twelve-hour shifts as it is.'

'Do you need me to come back?' Jamie had asked. 'I still have a couple of weeks left to do here, but perhaps if I explain, they'll let me go earlier.' Even as Jamie had asked the question he had known it wasn't that simple. If it hadn't been for Sarah and Calum he would have already booked the first plane back. He would have hated to let the Glasgow hospital down, but it was far easier for them to find a replacement than the small, poorly funded hospital in Africa.

'No, we can manage for another couple of weeks. Just. As long as we know you'll be coming, we can soldier on.'

'If you're sure?' Jamie said, not really convinced. 'You will let me know if it all becomes too much?'

'Straight away, I promise,' was the reply.

'How's Sibongele?' Jamie asked. 'Is he behaving himself?'

Again there was a slight hesitation. 'He's OK, I guess. He misses you. He asks every day when you're coming back.'

'Any news of family yet?'

'We're still trying to track down his mother's sister. One of the nurses thinks she knows which village she lives in and we have sent word to her that Sibongele is well enough to leave the hospital and go home. But so far we haven't heard anything. We don't even know if she got the message.'

'If we haven't heard by the time I get back, I'll go to the village myself and try and find her. The boy needs to be with his family.'

'The trouble is, Jamie, I don't think he wants to go. You know he thinks of you as his family since his mother died. He's been at the hospital for so long now, he doesn't remember anything else. He loves helping in the wards. He's bright and recites everything he's learnt from you at the drop of the hat.' Greg laughed. 'I swear some of the patients trust his opinion more than they do ours.'

Jamie smiled, too. He could easily picture fourteen-year-old Sibongele working on the wards with his ready smile and keenness to help. But he was a little concerned at how attached the boy had become to him. Heaven knew why the boy thought he could be a father to him—he couldn't even be sure he could be a father to his own child. But since the child had lost his mother to the TB that had kept Sibongele in the hospital for the past six months, he had developed an attachment to Jamie. And, Jamie had to admit, he was fond of the boy. In fact, although he was keen to see the boy reunited with his aunt, he knew he would miss him when he left.

After he replaced the receiver, Jamie prowled around his small flat. He felt restless and ill at ease. Once or twice he reached for the phone to call Sarah, but pulled back at the last minute. What, after all, could he say to her?

Jamie had always paid little heed to his sur-roundings, but today the one bed-roomed apartment seemed to closing in on him. As hospital accommodation went, it was clean and modern with an open-plan sitting room divided by a breakfast bar and a functional kitchenette. The rest of the flat comprised a boxy bedroom and a tiny bathroom with overhead shower.

A steady downpour of rain rattled the window-panes, dampening his spirits even further, and he experienced a sudden yearning for Africa.

As he thought of the country he had spent the last year and a half in, he realised how much he was missing the wide open spaces, and the mission hospital with the staff and patients. They would be struggling to cope without him. There were already too few doctors for too many patients. For a moment he let himself imagine what it would be like to return there with Sarah at his side. She would love the country, he was certain, and as for Calum, he would love it, too. There was an old reservoir that the staff used for dips. He could teach his son to swim. He pushed the thoughts away. It was unlikely to happen. Perhaps he should return sooner than he had planned? Hand in his notice and leave as soon as the hospital managed to find another locum to replace him? There was probably little requirement to further brush up his skills. Even the short time he had spent at the Royal was sufficient for him to be reassured that his clinical skills were fully up to date.

Why not, then? Why not just go? Remove himself from Sarah and Calum's lives? Let them get on with their lives.

The ringing of the phone rang dragged him away from his brooding thoughts.

'Hi. It's Robert. Can you meet me in the pub across the road in ten minutes?'

'Have you got the results?' Jamie felt his heart begin to beat faster. 'If you have, tell me now, over the phone.'

'Yes, I have the results. But I want to tell you face to face. Can you meet me or not?'

'Do I have an option?'

'Not really. See you in ten.' Jamie heard the click as Robert terminated the call.

As Jamie made the short walk to the pub, his mind was in turmoil. What if the results were positive? How would that affect Calum? He couldn't bear the distress it would cause Sarah when she learned that her child might have a disease that would severely limit her child's future. Would she agree to have him tested? What if she chose to wait until he was old enough to make his own decision? Perhaps his son would choose not to know. Follow in his father's footsteps? Well, he could hardly blame him. If the results were positive, Jamie knew that it was likely he could develop the illness at any time. How could he continue to be part of Calum's life knowing that one day he might become dependent on his child? He shuddered. Anything but that. He would have no option but to remove himself as quickly as possible from their lives. They would forget about him. Make their own future. In time Sarah would find someone else, someone who would be a good father to Calum and a support to her. Despite himself he felt his mind reel away from the image of Sarah in someone else's arms, in someone else's bed. Still, there was no point in torturing himself. In a few minutes he would know his fate.

He swung the pub door open, bringing a blast of cold air into the heavy atmosphere of the bar. It was almost empty apart from one or two couples enjoying their drinks at the small tables set out near the fire. Robert, a solitary figure at the bar, was already in the process of ordering drinks.

'That was quick. What can I get you?' he asked as Jamie approached.

'I could do with a large malt, but as I'm on call, a Coke will have to do.' Jamie waited impatiently. It seemed to take an interminable time for the barman to pour their drinks. He had to stop himself from hauling Robert off the barstool and demanding a response. Eventually they were both seated far away from listening ears in a secluded corner.

'Come on man. Spit it out,' Jamie ground out between clenched teeth.

Ignoring his tone, Robert raised his glass and grinned. 'Cheers.' he said. 'You can relax. The results were negative. You don't carry the gene.'

Jamie felt as if all the breath had been knocked out of his body. He had hardly dared to hope.

'You're sure?' he queried. 'I have to be a hundred per cent certain.'

'I knew you would feel like that, so I used my influence and got them to run the test twice. There's no doubt, you definitely do not have the gene.'

'Thank God for that.' He leant back in the chair. The relief was overwhelming. Now he knew, he could hardly take it all in.

'Hey, you owe me one,' Robert said with a smile of pleasure. 'I can't tell you how many favours I had to call in to get this done. And so quickly.'

'Anything you want. You just name it and it's yours,' Jamie responded fervently. 'Thank you. You have no idea what this means.' As the two men sat in silence Jamie's first thought was for his child. If he didn't have the gene, there was no chance that his son would have it either. Calum was never going to develop Huntington's chorea. He would never know the agony of having his muscles gradually lose control, with the subsequent loss of independence. He would never—as Jamie's father had done in the latter stages of the disease—

struggle with the simplest tasks of eating and breathing. There was nothing stopping Calum from having the brightest future.

His thoughts turned to himself. Neither would he know or have to suffer the effects of the devastating illness. He, too, was free to live his life like any other man. Free to love, have children. For the first time since he had learned of his father's illness as a third-year medical student, Jamie knew he had a future. And what would that future hold? Calum certainly. But could that future also include Sarah? Could she learn to trust him again? Fall in love with him once more? Or was it too late? Jamie knew that he had to find out. He needed to see her. Tell her everything. Make her understand why he had acted as he had.

Although he was desperate to talk to Sarah, good manners prevented him from jumping to his feet and leaving his friend to finish his drink alone.

'Can I get you another one?' he offered.

'No, thanks. I can tell you are straining at the bit to get away. Now you know, what are you going to do? Are you going to tell Sarah?'

'At least now I can explain why I behaved as I did. Hell, what must she think of me? First of all I rush away to Africa without a reasonable explanation and then when I return and find out I have a son, I appear to reject him, too. She must think I'm a real bastard.'

'Mmm, I see what you mean. But Sarah is a reasonable woman. Hopefully she'll understand. I suspect, though, that you're going to have to do a fair bit of grovelling first. Anyway, let's finish our drinks and get out of here. It's about time you got on with the rest of your life.'

Jamie felt too restless to go back to the residence. He needed to see Calum and Sarah and he needed to see them straight away. But first he'd pop into the department and make sure there were no patients requiring his expertise. It would mean he was less likely to be interrupted when he saw Sarah.

Jamie used the back entrance of the A and E department, walking past a thankfully empty resus suite. Glancing into the waiting room, he noted a scattering of people sitting patiently while they waited to be seen. Deciding to check the triage area before he left, he noted with surprise a familiar figure sitting at the nurses' station, chatting with Elspeth.

'Dr Campbell, hi—thought you were at home. I was just about to phone you. You have a visitor,' Elspeth explained, tilting her head in the direction of Mrs MacLeod.

'Mrs MacLeod! Is everything all right?' Jamie asked, frowning, wondering if her broken leg was causing her problems.

The elderly lady beamed up at him. 'Och, I'm just grand! Here, this is for you—baked it myself,' she added, holding out a biscuit tin which held a fresh-baked sponge cake. 'I wanted to show you how well I'm doing—and to thank you for everything you did.'

Aware that they were gathering an audience of nursing and medical staff, Jamie shifted uneasily. 'That was really kind of you, Mrs MacLeod. Thank you. But I was just doing my job, you know.'

'Rubbish, young man. What you did for me was way and beyond the call of duty and everyone knows it!' Getting stiffly to her feet, she leaned on her walking stick. 'Well, don't want to take up any more of your valuable time, Doctor. I need to be getting back to let in the home help, although to be honest she's a bit hopeless. It should be me taking care of her!'

Jamie smiled and shook his head in amazement at the spirit and courage of the elderly lady as she walked straight backed down the corridor. Noting the amused expressions of his colleagues gathered round the desk, he turned to Elspeth.

'As you all have nothing better to do than hover about here, I'm off. If you need me you can either page me or call my mobile.'

'Aren't you going to share your cake with us, Doctor?' Elspeth called after his departing back.

Jamie decided to walk the couple of miles to see Sarah. The fresh air and exercise would help clear his head. If the hospital called and he was needed urgently, he would flag a taxi and would be back at the hospital in no time.

Sarah was just finishing giving Calum his bath before getting him ready for bed when the doorbell rang. She wrapped the baby up in a soft white towel and carried him to the door. She expected to see either her mother or one of her friends. What she hadn't expected was Jamie, grinning broadly, holding what seemed to be a cake tin in his hand.

'Hello, you,' he said softly. 'Can I come in?'

He took in the sight of Sarah with their son in her arms. She was barefoot and wearing a pair of faded jeans with a broad leather belt low on her hips. Her white T-shirt rode up slightly, revealing her toned, lightly tanned abdomen. She had her hair tied up in a high ponytail and a blob of foam clung to her fringe. Jamie had never seen her look so desirable. He resisted the urge to pull her into his arms and cover her with kisses.

'As you can see, we are a little tied up at the moment. It's not really a convenient time,' she responded.

Jamie paid no attention to her frosty tone, instead stepping into the flat and taking Calum from her.

'I'll help you put him to bed, if you like.'

Sarah resisted the temptation to pluck Calum back. She refused to treat her child like a ping-pong ball. But who exactly did Jamie think he was? One minute he wanted nothing to do with her or her child, except perhaps a quick romp in the sack with her, and the next minute he was turning up at her door as if he lived there. The man had a nerve.

'What are you doing here, Jamie? If it's Calum you've come to see, we really need to discuss access.'

'You and I need to talk,' Jamie said firmly. 'But let's get this little one off to bed and then we can talk undisturbed. Just tell me what to do.' He had the grace to look a little self-conscious as he said that. Clearly Jamie had no idea what putting a baby to bed actually entailed.

Sarah suppressed a smile. It was an unusual situation, seeing Jamie in a position where he obviously felt clueless. This was completely different to how he normally appeared. Whether at work or in the mountains, Jamie always looked like a man who knew exactly what he was doing.

'OK, you can stay for a while—just this once. We do need to talk about Calum so I suppose tonight is as good a time as any. First I need to finish drying him properly.'

Sarah had lit a fire against the cooling autumnal nights and she reclaimed her son before setting him down on the changing mat she had placed at a safe distance from the hearth. Using the towel, she carefully dried between the baby's toes and folds. Calum squealed with pleasure, kicking with delight in his naked freedom.

Jamie looked at the two figures he was already beginning to think of as his family. The soft light of the flames and the standard lamp cast a glow around the room, chasing the last of the shadows that had hung over him before. Now everything was as it should be, or it would be once he had explained everything. Already he regretted the months of Calum's life that he had missed. Why had he been such a fool? Why hadn't he had the guts to take the test earlier? He would have known that he was free to pursue Sarah and he would have been there for her throughout the pregnancy and birth. He could only begin to imagine how hurt she must've been to not have told him that she was pregnant. And if she had? What then? He would have told her the truth and probably tried to convince her to have a termination. He felt his blood run cold at the mere possibility that his child might never have been.

'Could you watch him? I'm just going to fetch his pyjamas and bottle.' Sarah asked.

She left Jamie crouched over Calum making faces that had her son—their son—smiling. She didn't quite know how she felt about Jamie being there. Had he decided that he wanted to be involved in his child's life after all? And if so, how did she feel about that? She rummaged in a drawer for Calum's pyjamas, pulling out her favourite pair. Tiny blue rabbits frolicked on a white background. She walked back to the sitting room. Jamie had lifted Calum onto his lap. The child fixed his large brown eyes on Jamie's. They seemed in a world of their own. Sarah felt her throat tighten as she took in the scene. She could no longer doubt the affection Jamie had for his child.

She went to the kitchen and tested the temperature of the bottle she had left warming. She had stopped breastfeeding when she had returned to work, but missed the closeness of having the skin-to-skin contact that breastfeeding had involved. Yet another sacrifice she had made in order to return to work. Had it been worth it? If she hadn't gone back to work when she had, would she have missed Jamie's return to the UK? Believing him still in Africa, would she ever have told him about his son? Even now she didn't know what she was going to do about Jamie. She could tell from the way that he looked at Calum that he was smitten. But as far as she knew, he was still planning to go back to Africa. It wouldn't be fair on her son to have a father who dipped in and out of his life. No, Jamie had some tough choices to make. She had to make him see that.

Calum was looking calm and settled when she retrieved him from Jamie and slipped his pyjamas on. His little body was warm from his bath and the fire. He sucked drowsily at the bottle, his eyes beginning to close in sleep. Jamie and Sarah sat quietly as Calum finished his drink and surrendered himself to sleep. Sarah popped him in his cot, turning on the nightlight and leaving the door slightly ajar in case he woke up. By the time she returned to the sitting room Jamie had stoked the fire, which blazed cheerfully. Her thoughts flew back to that last night before Jamie had left for Africa—the night their son had been conceived.

'OK, you can start. I assume you're here to talk about Calum?'

She could see that Jamie was struggling to find words. Perhaps he had come to tell her he was returning to Africa sooner than planned? Once more she felt her heart sink at the prospect. Could she really bear to lose him again?

'There is something I have to tell you,' Jamie began. 'If you can, please, hear me out before saying anything.'

Mutely Sarah nodded her head. Here it was. The goodbye scene all over again.

'My father died three years ago. You know

that. But what you didn't know was that he died from Huntington's chorea.'

Sarah couldn't help a gasp of surprise. Why hadn't he told her? Her heart began to race as she realised the full implications of Jamie's words.

'It's OK.' He rushed on, seeing Sarah's expression. 'I have just found out that I don't carry the gene. That's what I was doing when I took syringes and needles from the department.'

'Why on earth didn't you tell me before?'

'I couldn't, Sarah. I'm sorry. I decided a long time ago that I didn't want to know whether I carried the gene. I didn't want to lead my life knowing what could be in store for me. And I couldn't ask you to be with me for the same reason. What if I had it? I would never have allowed you to sacrifice your life to look after me. I would never have stopped you from having the children you so clearly wanted. And children weren't an option for me as long as I thought there was any chance I carried the gene and could pass it on.'

Sarah's mind reeled from what Jamie was telling her. Why couldn't he have told her? Had he that little faith in her? Of course he had always been protective of her, but this was too much. He should have trusted her. Her thoughts veered away from the thought of her son having a terminal illness. If she had known when she'd been pregnant, would she have gone through with the pregnancy? It would have been another thing to think of on top of the raised alpha fetoprotein. The possibility of her child having both genetic disorders might have been enough to make her reconsider going ahead. And if she hadn't? She felt ill.

'So you can see why I was horrified to discover that I had fathered a child. But once I knew, of course there was no option but for me to take the test.'

'You should have told me, Jamie. Why couldn't you have trusted me? Did you think my feelings were so shallow that I would run at the first sign of trouble?' she said sadly.

'It's because I knew you wouldn't run that I couldn't tell you. You would have stayed with me regardless. You are that type of woman and I couldn't have borne your pity.'

'Did you pity your father? Is that how your mother felt about him?'

'No, my mother loved my father. But it wasn't easy on her, watching him deteriorate in front of her, knowing she was helpless to prevent the illness from claiming him. She spent the last couple of years of his life as his full-time carer. She wouldn't let me employ nurses to help. Said my father's care was her responsibility. That she needed to be the one to look after him. But looking after him took its toil on her health, mental and physical.' Jamie took a ragged breath, remembering how his arguments and entreaties had fallen on deaf ears.

'Isn't that what love is about, Jamie?' Sarah said quietly. 'Isn't that what people promise when they take their vows—"in sickness and in health"?'

'That's just it. You would have made those vows. And stuck by them. No matter how trapped you felt. My mother had no life of her own. And, no, I didn't pity my father. I just felt helpless. What was the point of all those years of medical training if there was nothing I could do to help? So you see, I couldn't have a child. Not knowing if I'd end up a burden on them. Never mind the chances of them inheriting the disease. Rightly or wrongly, I made up my mind.'

'Did you think of your father as a burden?'

'It would have been a privilege to do anything for him. But he would never let me. He was a proud man. He would only let my mother look after him,' Jamie said, unable to disguise the pain in his voice.

'And you've found out that you're OK. What now?'

'Now we can be a family. A real family. You, me and Calum. Isn't that what you have always wanted?'

'Is it?' she said quietly. Jamie seemed oblivious to the ice in her tone.

'You and Calum can come back to Africa with me. You can give up work or work part time. You'll love it there. It'll give you all the time you want to spend with Calum.'

'And why would I do that? What about my life here? My work, my friends, my mother?'

'It'll only be for a couple of years at first.

Your mother and friends can come and visit.
And as for your work—you'll find the work in
Africa just as, if not more, rewarding.'

'I think you should leave now, Jamie,' Sarah
said softly.

He looked at her in surprise. Clearly this wasn't
the reaction he had been expecting. Suddenly
she couldn't hold back the anger any longer.

'You waltz in here, telling me that you have
decided that my son and I should give up our
lives and go back with you to Africa. You disappear from my life without any real explanation, leaving me to deal with pregnancy, birth
and looking after a small child on my own. OK,
OK.' She held up her hands to stop his
response. 'I know you didn't know I was
pregnant, but that's hardly the point, is it? You
could have made enquiries about me. We have
colleagues in common. Weren't you the slightest bit interested in how I was coping? In my
life—my career? Then you saunter back into
my life and nearly make love to me before rejecting me—again.' She stopped his words
again. 'OK, so I did give you some encourage-

ment. But you caught me at a weak moment. Then, after showing little interest in your son, you find out that he is hale and hearty after all. So it now suits you to have him in your life. But worst of all, instead of coming here, grovelling for forgiveness, you come in, demanding that I give up *my* life and follow you to Africa like some kind of…' She paused to draw breath. 'Some kind of groupie!' she spat finally. She stood, indicating the door. 'Now, before I say anything I might regret, I think you should leave, don't you?'

Well, Jamie thought as he walked back to his flat, that hadn't gone exactly as planned. He had to admit he had been so delighted that he didn't have the gene that he hadn't really stopped to think about Sarah's reaction. Of course it was bound to be a shock to her. He had been a blundering, insensitive fool. He should have broken the news more gently. Taken his time. Waited for the right moment. Considered his words. But, dammit, Sarah and his son were going to be a part of his future—his future in

Africa. Once more he mulled over what she had said, that she had made a life and a career for herself in Glasgow. Was he being fair to ask her to leave everything she had worked so hard to achieve? But there wasn't really an option. He was committed to at least another year of his contract and he couldn't leave Sibongele just yet—not until he knew that the boy's future was secure. There was so much Sarah could do in Africa. She would love it there—he was sure of it—if only she would give it and him a chance.

Jamie sighed. He would just have to use what little time he had left to convince her. He had forgotten what a prickly and stubborn soul she was. But he would be patient. He was pretty sure she still had feelings for him, although, he admitted ruefully, tonight she had kept them pretty well hidden if she still did. He gave a wry smile as he thought back to the image of Sarah standing in front of him, cheeks blazing. She had always been a passionate woman. Not least in bed. And he was determined that shortly she'd be back where she belonged. Back in his bed and his life. But this time for good.

CHAPTER SEVEN

THE day of Lizzie's wedding dawned cool but clear. Autumn was turning into winter, the trees scattering carpets of gold, bronze and red everywhere. The sun shone on one of those perfect crisp days that drew visitors to Scotland from all over the world.

Sarah had spent the last couple of days mulling over what Jamie had told her. Once she had cooled down, she allowed herself to feel a little sympathy for Jamie's predicament. It must have been terrible to live your life not knowing what the future held in store. And to watch the deterioration of the health, physical and mental, of someone you loved, knowing that despite your medical training you were powerless to do anything, must have been awful for a man like Jamie.

If he had told her, what would she have done? He was right in one respect. She would never have left him. She would have tried to persuade him to have the test, and if it had been positive she would have given up her dream of having children. She had loved him that much. But had he loved her? Surely if he had, he would have fought for a life together. He could never have simply have walked away from her without at least having the courage to find out whether they could have a future.

But to be fair, she could understand why Jamie had kept the truth from her. He wasn't the kind of man who would have allowed anyone to sacrifice their life. Still, it hadn't been only his decision to make. He should have trusted her. If he had loved her enough, surely he would have? At least found out whether he had the gene before deciding to give her up.

And now—did he really want to be part of her life, or was it just Calum he was interested in? And should that not be enough? Did she have the right to deny her son the chance to know his father? But Jamie hadn't said anything about staying. From what she could gather, he still intended to go back to Africa. With or without her and Calum.

Jamie hadn't sought her out over the last couple of days. The department had been busy and there were always other staff about. But surely he could have tried harder to see her and Calum in the evenings? Or was he waiting, respecting her need for time before he put any more pressure on her?

She didn't know the answer to any of her questions. She felt exhausted from the sleepless nights where she had lain tossing and turning, trying to decide what to do.

Reluctantly Sarah had allowed her mother to persuade her to go to Lizzie's wedding reception.

'You need some fun, darling,' she had coaxed. 'Some time to enjoy yourself. You're not doing yourself or Calum any good by working so hard.'

Most days, it had been all Sarah could do to get herself home in time to play with Calum before feeding him, bathing him and putting him to bed. Once he was in bed, Sarah usually had energy only for a light snack, before stumbling off to bed herself. No wonder she was losing weight.

Lizzie had added her entreaties to those of Sarah's mum. 'I've spoken to Jean and invited her, too. She's suggested that she come for a couple of hours and then take Calum home with her so that you can relax and enjoy the rest of the evening. All you'll be missing of Calum is the time he's usually asleep.' She had peered into Sarah's face, noting the dark circles under her eyes. 'You've been working too hard, girl. You deserve a break.' She had searched Sarah's eyes. 'Or is there something else? Something bothering you? Do you need to talk? You know, Sarah, I've been so caught up in wedding arrangements I haven't being paying attention to anyone else.'

Sarah had grown increasingly fond of Lizzie in the time she had known her. Since she had decided to confide in her, the young nurse and Sarah had become firm friends, finding that they shared the same sense of humour as well as a work ethic. She hadn't told her about Jamie and the reason he had given her for leaving. There hadn't really been the opportunity.

'I know I can talk to you. And I will when the time is right. But not now, Lizzie. If you don't mind?'

Lizzie hadn't pressed her further. Sarah had known it was important to Lizzie that she be there on her special day and so finally had agreed with her mother's suggestion.

She had been unsure of what to wear, finally settling on a knee-length red silk evening dress, the soft fabric draping her curves, crossing sexily at the back. It was trimmed with contrasting velvet ribbon that tied under the bust and emphasised the gentle swell of her breasts. She added a small cashmere bolero with long sleeves that would protect her against the cool evening air. After further thought she had decided to wear her designer sandals with the impossibly high heels. She could always kick them off for dancing if need be, but she had sacrificed enough by wearing flat shoes at work. The shoes deserved an outing and she deserved a glamorous look after the months of casual attire and conservative workwear. Sarah had every intention of getting at least a couple of dances in. How long had it been since she had danced?

She left her hair loose with a parting to the side. A rare visit to the hairdresser ensured that it lay perfectly straight and glossy. She had gone for the glam look with her make-up, too. Instead of the usual quick slick of lipstick, she coated her already long lashes with mascara and added just a touch of eye-shadow that brought out the green of her eyes.

'If I could wolf whistle, I would,' her mother said appreciatively when Sarah emerged from her bedroom. 'You look stunning. Can I ask,' she added with a twinkle, 'if all this is for the benefit of anyone in particular?'

Sarah had told her mother about Jamie. Jean had surprised her by supporting Jamie's decision. 'It explains a lot about his behaviour. Perhaps it wasn't the right decision but, knowing the kind of man he is, I can see why it was the one he made.'

'Getting dressed up is for *my* benefit, Mum.

To be honest, I've forgotten what it feels like to be a woman again. I love being a mother, but for once it feels good to be me again.' But, Sarah had to admit, there was a part of her that wanted Jamie to see her looking her best. He, too, was going to the wedding. Although in theory it was his weekend on, management had agreed to employ one of the retired consultants to cover two weekends in four. It had long been agreed that there was too much work in the department for two consultants and, apart from old Dr MacDonald's replacement, the hospital was actively seeking to recruit a third.

Calum had had his afternoon nap and was buttoned up in his padded suit and hat in his car seat. They would be taking two cars so that Jean could take Calum home with her. His cheeks were still rosy from his nap and when he saw his mother, he squirmed and smiled, blowing bubbles. She knew how lucky she was to have such a contented baby. She had heard so many horror stories about babies who never slept or never stopped crying.

'Come on, then, darling,' she said to her son,

picking him up in his car seat. 'Let's get this show on the road. Do you want to follow me, Mum?'

'Don't worry. I know my way there,' Jean replied. 'You get going and I'll be along in a bit.'

Sarah enjoyed the half-hour car journey out to the hotel, which was situated on the shores of Loch Lomond. Within a few minutes they had left the city behind and were in the countryside. The sun was just sinking in the sky, bathing everything in a dusky pink light. The wind had dropped and on her left Sarah could see the water of Loch Lomond reflecting the trees that protected its banks. In the distance, the hills of the Highlands already had a dusting of snow on their tops and Sarah looked forward to a time when she could take her son hill walking. As she sang to keep Calum amused, she remembered the many weekends she and Jamie had spent climbing and hill walking. She thought of exhilarating excursions followed by early nights in cosy hotels with log fires in the winter and stunning views in the summer. She had enjoyed hunting down the best places to stay. Neither of them had cared for the anonymity of the large hotel chains. After dinner and a couple of drinks, she and Jamie would beat a hasty retreat to their room where they had expended any leftover energy making love until finally, exhausted, they'd fallen asleep…

When they drew up at the impressive grounds of the hotel, night was beginning to fall and the hotel was lit up like a fairy castle. Calum looked at the lights, his eyes stretched in awe. As she carried him over, Elspeth rushed over to greet her and fuss over the baby.

Sarah relinquished Calum to the older woman. 'Aren't you just the most darling baby?' she crooned.

'Most of the time he is,' Sarah agreed, 'but he does have his moments. Were you at the ceremony, Elspeth? Did all go well?'

'Without a hitch. Lizzie looks absolutely breathtaking, as you'll see for yourself. She loves her wedding dress so much she's going to keep it on for the whole evening. And Stewart looked very handsome, too. As he requested, all the men are in kilts—including our own Dr Campbell. Most of the folk who have been invited for the reception are here already. They're in the bar, if you want to catch up with them.'

'I think I'll just take Calum for a look around the grounds before the light fades completely. I've never been here before. Could you let my mother know where we are when she arrives? We won't be long.'

Sarah was forced to keep to the paths, her high heels preventing her from cutting across the lawn. Calum was getting heavy in her arms and she looked forward to the time when he'd be able to toddle. She breathed in the air, filled with the scent of roses. It felt so good to be outside away from the smog and the confines of the city, even for a short time. Until tonight, she hadn't realised how much she missed spending time in the country. She looked up as she heard footsteps crunching the gravel behind her. Jamie, dressed in his kilt—Sarah recognised the Campbell tartan—was making his way towards them. He wore a dress shirt and tweed jacket with a *skean dubh* tucked in his dress socks. On anyone else the frilly shirt might have looked effeminate but on Jamie's muscular frame and with his dark eyes and hair, Sarah could only think of William Wallace, the famous Scottish hero. For one moment she let herself imagine being swept up in Jamie's arms and being carried away to some Highland bothy, where he would ravish her. Or she him, she admitted to herself as she felt a hot wave of desire wash over her.

'Here, let me take Calum,' her Highland hero said instead.

'I-I've never s-seen you in a kilt before,' Sarah stammered, not wanting him to see how affected she was by her fantasies.

'I've resisted up until tonight. But Lizzie insisted and I couldn't let her down on her big day, could I?' He tossed Calum into the air, making him squeal with delight. 'And how are you, young man?'

'I thought you didn't approve of babies at weddings,' Sarah reminded him.

Jamie had the grace to look a little shame-faced. 'I'm sorry. You were right. I had no right to tell you how to bring up your son. Not after you had the burden of bringing him up on your own. So, Sarah, have you had to think about things? Are you going to let me shoulder at least some of the responsibility?'

'He's never been a burden,' Sarah retorted, more sharply than she'd intended. 'Hard work perhaps, but never a burden. And if that's how you see him then—'

'Hey. Cool it. I didn't mean it like that. It's just that it must be hard going. Working all the hours that God sends and then caring for this little chap on top of everything.'

It was Sarah's turn to look a little shame-faced. 'I'm sorry. But, no, I haven't decided yet. That all rather depends on you.' The evening was turning cool and whether it was the night air or some premonition that made Sarah shiver, she couldn't be sure.

'Let's go inside—you look frozen. Here, take this,' Jamie said. Juggling Calum in one arm, he removed his jacket and wrapped it around Sarah's shoulders.

'Sarah, I need to go back to Africa. They depend on me. If you could only see it for yourself, you'd understand. Why don't you and Calum come for a couple of weeks?'

'It won't make any difference, Jamie. Don't you understand? I can't—won't—give up everything I've worked for, my career, my family, to go with you. It's too early for us to know whether we have a future. I thought I knew you and I was wrong. I'm just not prepared to take a chance.'

Jamie looked at her intently. 'But I can't stay here—can't you see that? I'm under contract and they are so short-staffed it would be almost negligent to resign anyway. And there's someone—a young boy—I promised I would look after.' He tilted her chin and gazed down at her. 'Give us a chance, SJ,' he said quietly, his voice thick with emotion. 'I know I was a fool, a coward even, to leave you without telling you my reasons, but I thought it was for the best. Can't you see I was just trying to protect you?'

Sarah shook her head sadly. 'That's just the problem, Jamie. You treated me as if I were a child. Not a grown woman who had the right to make her own decisions. And now you are asking me to trust *you* enough to risk every-thing I've worked so hard for?'

Jamie looked into the distance. 'I guess, then, that I have no option but to try and work some-thing out. I'll do whatever it takes to be with you and Calum.'

At his words Sarah felt as if a weight had been lifted from her shoulders. For a moment she allowed herself to feel a surge of happiness.

She looked into the face knew almost as well as her own. She longed to reach out and trace the lines around his mouth, creases that she knew were caused by laughter. But she didn't trust herself to touch him. 'How can I be sure you don't want me just because of Calum?'

'Good grief, woman. I know you'd never stop me seeing Calum whenever I like. Obviously I'd rather be with him all the time, but in the meantime I'll take what I can. But make no mistake, SJ. I want you, too. And not simply because you're the mother of my child. We had something once, and could have it again if only you'll give us another try.'

Sarah desperately wanted to believe him.

Could she trust him again? Take a risk that he meant what he said? That he wasn't staying just because of Calum? If only she could be sure.

'Can we take one day at a time? See what happens?'

'I'll do whatever it takes. I don't intend to lose you again. Come on, let's go and join the party.'

Inside, the dancing had started. The band, which consisted of a couple of fiddlers, an accordion player, a drummer and a singer, was playing the wedding waltz and Lizzie and her new husband were dancing to it, cheek to cheek.

Elspeth hadn't exaggerated. Lizzie looked radiant in her ivory silk dress with sweetheart neckline and antique pearl buttons. Her rich auburn hair, swept up into a flattering chignon, was the perfect foil for the coronet of miniature roses.

The room in which the reception was being held had high ceilings with ornate cornicing and ceiling roses. Long velvet curtains graced the enormous windows that stretched from floor to ceiling. Tables to accommodate the buffet and chairs were set out, while comfy sofas were stationed in strategic positions to allow revellers the opportunity to rest their feet. Beyond the opened French doors, a patio overlooked the loch. Sarah could make out the distant lights of small boats as they berthed for the night.

Taking advantage of a break in the dancing, Sarah went over to congratulate the happy couple.

'I just wish everyone could experience the happiness that I feel today.' Lizzie looked pointedly at Sarah and then looked over at Jamie, who was moving towards them, making her meaning clear. 'Make the most of your time out, Sarah, and enjoy the dancing.' As Lizzie and Stewart rushed off to greet some late arrivals, Jamie walked up to Sarah.

'May I have the pleasure of this dance?' he asked formally, then, noticing her gaze sweeping the room for her son, he added, 'Don't worry about Calum. He's having a great time being fussed over by the staff. And your mum has found a kindred spirit in Elspeth.'

What the hell, thought Sarah. Now she was here she was determined to have a good time. 'I'd be delighted,' she said with a small curtsy, equalling his formality. 'Just let me kick off these heels first.'

They joined several others who had lined up for Strip the Willow. As the dancers swirled to the music, Sarah began to relax and enjoy herself. Jamie was surprisingly light on his feet for someone so tall and muscular. But climbers had to be agile as well as strong. Every time they met in the middle Sarah was acutely aware of his powerful arms clasping hers.

'Whew!' Sarah laughed as the dance came to an end. 'I had forgotten how much energy Scottish country dancing takes. I need to cool down.'

'So do I, 'said Jamie, a mischievous glint in his eye. 'Let's go out on the patio for a while.'

As he led her out, Sarah continued, 'I'm seriously unfit. I desperately need to make time for some exercise.'

'I'm going climbing tomorrow. Why don't you come with me?'

For a moment Sarah was tempted. The drive up had made her realise how desperately she had missed the mountains. 'Who else is going?'

'I'm going on my own. None of my old climbing buddies were free so I decided to go anyway.'

Sarah looked at him. 'You shouldn't be going on your own. What if something happens? Who is going to belay for you?'

'I don't need anyone. You know I've climbed on my own a hundred times. Besides, if you come with me I won't be on my own, will I?'

'I'm afraid emotional blackmail isn't going to work. And, besides, haven't you forgotten something?'

'Calum. Actually, I've already spoken to your mum. She thinks it's a great idea for you to have a day off. She and Elspeth are busy hatching a plan for Calum tomorrow.'

'Does Elspeth know..?'

'That I'm Calum's father? I'm not sure. I certainly haven't told anyone—although you know I'd be proud to acknowledge him as my son, I rather think that's your decision, don't you?'

'Yes, it is. I'm not sure at this stage whether there is any need for anyone to know.'

Jamie left the unspoken question hang in the

air. 'Think about it at least. It will give us some uninterrupted time together for once,' he said as a group of guests spilled onto the patio.

The rest of the evening passed all too quickly. Jean had told Sarah she was taking a sleepy Calum home after a couple of hours. 'I don't know about him, but I'm ready for my bed.' Sarah had cast a worried look at her mother.

'If you're feeling tired, Mum, I'll come, too. I'm quite happy to leave. After all, I've managed a couple of dances.'

'And spoil your first night out in months? No, I don't think so.'

'I don't want you driving back on your own if you're tired.'

Jamie came up just in time to hear the last of the conversation. 'Look, I have a room booked here for the night. I thought it would be more convenient for an early start on the hills in the morning. Jean and Calum could take it for the night.'

'It's very kind of you, Jamie,' Jean replied, 'but we couldn't possibly put you out.'

'I think its easier all round if I just take Mum

and Calum home. Calum needs his routine,' Sarah interjected. 'Especially in the morning. Besides, I didn't bring enough nappies and bottles for overnight. Thanks for the offer, Jamie, but I'll just go and fetch my coat.'

'Stop right there,' Jamie said in a voice that Sarah knew well. 'Your mother is quite right. You need a night off. You stay and enjoy yourself. I'll take your mother and Calum home. It's the least I can do,' he finished with a pointed look at Sarah. But his look held something else. Almost supplication. Sarah knew what he was really demanding. That she let him help. 'It'll only take me forty minutes to get there and back,' Jamie continued. 'I'll be back before the band finishes, so don't give away the last dance to anyone else.'

'All right,' she agreed reluctantly, wondering if she was making the right decision. 'We can collect your car in the morning, Mum. If you want to sleep in my room, I'll take the sofa so I won't disturb you when I come in.'

'I'll just take Calum through to mine,' Jean said. 'I've got everything there he needs, including a travel cot. It will give you a chance for a lie-in. Unless you're going climbing with Jamie in the morning?'

Sarah caught the conspiratorial look that passed between Jamie and her mother. If they thought they were going to outmanoeuvre her they were very much mistaken.

'I'm not going climbing tomorrow. I simply don't want to leave Calum for a whole day when I can help it—not yet. Maybe another time, though,' she conceded.

'Perhaps the three of us could do something together tomorrow instead. I can leave the climb for another time,' Jamie suggested.

This was different. If Jamie was prepared to put his child's needs before his own, it was a start.

'I'll think about it. Let you know before the end of the night?'

'OK, you two,' Jamie said 'Let's get going. Can we take your car, Jean? I somehow don't think I can manage two adults and a baby seat in a sports car.'

Another change Jamie was going to have to make if he was to take up his paternal responsibilities—the sports car would have to go. Sarah couldn't help a smile of satisfaction. Jamie was going to find out pretty soon what being a parent was really like.

On the way back from dropping off Jean and Calum, Jamie knew he had one thing left to do. He pulled over into a layby, and picking up his mobile, dialled the international number he knew from memory. After a pause filled with clicks and whirs, a distorted voice answered the phone.

'Lebowa Hospital. How may I direct your call?'

'Dr Lawson, please.' Jamie had to wait another couple of minutes before Greg, his friend and colleague, answered.

'Jamie. Delighted to hear your voice. I hope you're ringing to tell us you're coming back sooner than expected.'

'Actually, Greg, I'm sorry to disappoint you, but I was calling to let you know that I've decided to apply for a permanent position here. I'll be coming back for a week or two, at least until you find someone to replace me and to see

Sibongele settled, but after that I'm afraid you're on your own. I'll explain everything when I see you.'

There was a short silence on the other end of the phone.

'I'm sorry to hear that, James. But I'm sure you've got your reasons. I don't have to tell you how disappointed we will be to lose you. We need all the doctors of your calibre and experience we can get.'

'I know, Greg. If there was any other way... If you like, I can try and recruit someone for you this side.'

'That would be a help. The sooner the better, and at least we'll have you back for a short while, but, James, I was just about to phone you. There's something else...'

'What is it? Is Sibongele all right?'

Jamie could hear Greg's deep sigh over the crackling of the phone.

'Actually, he's not. We finally traced his aunt and she won't take him. Says she has too many other mouths to feed, and I can't say I blame her. The trouble is, when we told Sibongele that he'd have to go into care, he became very distressed. Said he wanted to stay with you. We explained that that wasn't possible, and he'd have to go. So he ran away. We found him eventually, poor boy, frozen and frightened, and took him back to the hospital, but he says he'll run away from the home if we make him go. There's no talking to him. He just keeps asking for you. Says you'll make everything all right.'

Jamie rubbed a weary hand across his face. Poor Sibongele. He'd known so many losses in his short life—first his mother from the tuberculosis that had kept the child in hospital for the past six months, and now his aunt. And although he didn't know it yet, he was about to lose *him,* too. Jamie had promised the young boy he'd stay in touch if he went to live with his aunt. But how could he keep his promise now? Sibongele would never understand why he, too, appeared to be deserting him.

'How is he now?'

'He's not saying much, except to ask when you'll be back.'

'Look, don't say anything to him about me leaving until I have time to think. I need to be the one to tell him.'

Jamie thought for a moment. 'My locum here finishes at the end of next week. I'll try and get a flight out after that. Keep trying to find someone to replace me in the meantime, and I'll do my best to find someone this end.'

'Any help or time you could give us would be gratefully received. Thank you.'

The two men spent the next few minutes talking about the hospital before saying their goodbyes. At Jamie's request, Greg put Sibongele on the phone for a couple of minutes.

'Hello,' Sibongele greeted him. 'When are you coming home?'

'I'll be coming soon, Sibongele. We'll talk then. But in the meantime you must promise me that you won't run away again.'

'Only if I can stay with you.'

Jamie's heart sunk. How could he make a promise that he couldn't possibly keep? Jamie knew, despite the stoicism that Sibongele had always shown through his long recovery, the fourteen-year-old would be devastated to lose him too..

'Just promise me, Sibongele. No more running away.'

'OK. Until you come back. I like it here at the hospital. They are teaching me at the school. If I learn, maybe I, too, can become a doctor. Dr Greg and the others are letting me help and they say I am quick to learn.'

'I know you are a good worker and a good student.' Jamie thought for a moment. Was there a chance he could arrange for Sibongele to study in the UK? He would need to find out before he raised the boy's hopes.

As Jamie ended the call, he felt torn. He'd have to go back, at least until they'd found someone to replace him and he knew that Sibongele was all right. Sarah would understand when he explained, and it wouldn't be for ever, a couple of months perhaps, maybe a little longer, and then he could return to be with them both for good.

Before Sarah knew it, Jamie had arrived back. She had danced non-stop in the hour he had been away and her feet were beginning to ache. She had noticed that Karen and Keith were dancing a lot together and wondered if she was witnessing the beginnings of a new romance. Or had it being going on for some time and she had been too preoccupied to notice? Whatever, she was pleased for them. They suited each other, the vivacious Karen acting as a foil to Keith's more serious nature. She hoped that if they were involved with one another, their romance would run more smoothly than hers and Jamie's had.

'Is this dance taken?' a deep voice said in her ear. She looked up to find Jamie looking down at her, his eyes glinting. Without waiting for a reply, he led her onto the dance floor, where the band were playing a waltz to slow down the tempo and bring the evening to a close.

Jamie held Sarah close to his chest as they moved to the music. She could feel the steady beat of his heart and the hard muscle beneath her hands as she slid her arms around his back. He pulled her nearer.

'Did I tell you how beautiful you look

tonight?' he said huskily, sliding his hands down her bare back to the point where her bottom curved.

She felt the flames of desire course through her body. She could smell the faint whiff of aftershave and the familiar scent was intoxicating her senses. He bent his head to hers and for a moment she thought he was going to kiss her. Right there in front of their colleagues.

'Let's get out of here,' he growled instead, and, taking her hand, led her out of the door into the grounds. He found a secluded spot underneath a sweeping oak tree, before pulling her once again into his arms.

'God, I've missed you,' he murmured before claiming her mouth.

She kissed him back hungrily, allowing the months of anger and hurt to disappear. What did it matter if he left her again? Her need for him right now was too strong. Tomorrow could wait.

He caressed her face, her breasts with urgent hands. 'Stay with me tonight, SJ. Please. Stay.'

She felt helpless to resist him. She nodded imperceptibly and he led her back inside. She was barely aware of the other guests as they passed through the foyer. He led her up the stairs, too impatient to wait for a lift to take them up the couple of flights. He had barely time to close the door behind them before they were once more in each other's arms, tearing at each others clothes in their desperate need.

Within seconds she stood before him in her bra and panties. She had giggled as he had struggled out of his kilt, the unfamiliar garment becoming entangled in his feet in his haste. He had looked wounded at her laughter before pulling her onto the bed. 'Hell, don't look at me like that, woman,' he said hoarsely before finishing the removal of her silk underwear with a proficiency that left her breathless.

Naked before him, she was suddenly shy. His eyes raked her body and she felt herself tingle with the blatant desire she could see there. He placed his hands gently on her hips, circling her hip bones with his thumb. She shuddered as he raised a hand and cupped her breast. Hot flames of desire licked her body and she groaned, leaning into his touch. He let his hands travel downwards towards, stroking the soft flesh at the tops of her legs. She moaned with her need for him. She wanted him inside her, filling the void that was within her. Now! She couldn't wait any longer. It was his turn to gasp as she reached for him and guided him into her, sitting on his lap, her legs astride his. As he filled her she stopped for a moment. He took her face in his hands and they stared into each other's eyes. Then, involuntarily, she began to move her hips against him. He grasped her buttocks, support-ing her until finally they both allowed their release to claim them. As they lay in each other's arms, spent, Sarah cuddled into his shoulder.

She didn't want to talk about the future or the past. All she wanted was to remain there with him and pretend the night would never end.

'Do you think anyone noticed our hasty de-parture?' she said, a smile in her voice.

'Don't give a damn if they did,' was the reply.

'We'll be a source of gossip throughout the

hospital by Monday if anyone did.' Sarah said with a sigh.

'You don't mind too much, do you?' said Jamie lazily, allowing his hands to travel over her body, refamiliarising himself with its contours.

Sarah felt herself grow warm as his hands travelled over her, feeling the new curves that motherhood had left. Self-consciously she pulled her stomach in, aware that it was no longer the flat one that he had known.

'Hey, I like the new curves,' Jamie protested, aware of her reaction. 'They suit you.' She felt his hand travel lower still and this time her intake of breath was in case he stopped. She couldn't bear it if he stopped.

After they'd had their fill of each other once more, Sarah climbed out of bed and began to get dressed.

'Where are you going?' Jamie asked, reaching to pull her back down next to him.

'I've got to get home,' Sarah said, pulling her dress on over her underwear. 'I know Calum is safe with my mother but I need to be at home just in case he wakes up and wants me. I'll creep in and put him back in his own cot. I know Mum said she'd keep him till morning but she already does enough. She looked tired tonight. I worry it's all too much for her.' She bent down to slip on her shoes.

Jamie started to get out of bed. 'I'll drive you home.'

'Don't be silly. How will you get your car?'

'I could stay the night with you and we could pick it up on our way out tomorrow,' Jamie suggested.

'I don't think so. I think we should take things slowly for a while,' Sarah said softly, pressing him back down and laughing as she avoided his reaching arms. She picked up her bag, and looked at Jamie once more. He was lying on his back, arms behind his head, grinning at her. She wanted nothing more at that moment than to crawl back next to him

'After all, we have all the time in the world now,' she added.

'SJ, there is something I want to talk to you about,' Jamie replied.

Something in his tone stopped her in her

tracks. Somehow she knew immediately that she didn't want to hear what he had to say.

'Sarah,' he said quietly. 'I'm sorry, but I have to go back…'

CHAPTER EIGHT

'GO BACK?' Sarah echoed, stunned.

'I made a phone call to Africa on my mobile while I was on my way back and—'

'But you said that you would do anything to be with Calum and me,' Sarah interrupted.

'And I meant it. But they need me—'

But Sarah was in no mood to let him finish. 'So what was all this, then?' She indicated the rumpled bed with a sweep of her hand. Suddenly she was furious. How could she have been so stupid? She should have known that Jamie would do anything in his power to achieve the result he wanted. He had clearly never intended to stay. What was it he had actually said? *I'll do anything to be with you and Calum.* Stupidly she had assumed that he'd meant he would be staying. But obviously he had never had any intention of not going back to Africa. Did he really think that all he had to do was seduce her and she'd give up everything, uproot her son and go with him to Africa?

'I want you and Calum to come with me.'

'And you thought that seducing me was the best way to persuade me to throw everything I've worked for away? That once I'd been back in your bed, I couldn't resist following you? Where was the discussion? When were my needs to be considered? Or Calum's, for that matter?'

'Hey, I haven't finished,' Jamie protested.

Incandescent with anger and something else—hurt and disappointment, not just for herself but for Calum—Sarah's eyes fell on Jamie's walking boots lying in a corner. Before she could stop herself she had grabbed one and flung it at him, narrowly missing his head.

'Oh, but I think you—we—are finished,' she said, turning on her heel. 'Don't even think about turning up at my place tomorrow. You can forget any *family* walks. From now on, if you want to see Calum you can arrange it through your solicitor, although how you are going to manage access from Africa is beyond me.'

And with a last final glare at Jamie, who was regarding her with disbelief, she closed the door behind her.

Sarah used her key to creep into her mother's flat. Calum lay on his back in the travel cot, arms flung above his head, abandoned in sleep. Her heart twisted as she looked down at her son while bending to smooth a lock of hair from his brow. What had he done to deserve a father who seemed as disinterested in him as hers had been in her?

Calum seemed a little warm to her so she removed a blanket. She was reluctant to disturb him by picking him up to take him back to her flat so she switched on the baby monitor beside his bed instead. That way, if he woke during the night, or in the early hours of the morning, she'd hear him and with a bit of luck would get to him before he woke her mother. She spent a few more minutes with Calum before returning to her flat.

Her heart thudded as she made out a tall figure standing by the front door. Instead of the kilt of the evening, Jamie was now dressed in faded jeans and a grey, thin, knit sweater.

'I'm tired, Jamie. Whatever it is you've come to say, it can wait till morning.'

'I wanted to make sure you got home OK. Besides, you didn't let me finish what I was saying back there. Thank God my reflexes are still good.' He smiled ruefully. 'You nearly got me a cracker.'

'Please, go, Jamie.' She felt her throat close. 'If you have any respect or regard for me at all, please, go.'

'Not until I finish telling you what you wouldn't let me back at the hotel.'

'I don't know what you could possibly have to say that will make any difference at all, but go on.'

'I thought I could stay. I really did, SJ, but I spoke to Greg, my colleague at the hospital tonight, and they are really desperate. But it's not just that. Something else has happened.'

As succinctly as possible Jamie told Sarah about the conversation he'd had with Greg.

'Don't you see, SJ? Sibongele really needs me right now. If I tell him I'm leaving for good, there is no telling what he'll do.'

'And Calum. Doesn't he need his father? I thought you promised, just a few hours ago, that you would never abandon him.'

Jamie pulled his hand through his hair. Sarah felt a pang of sympathy as she took in the lines of tiredness and regret.

'I meant what I said. I won't leave him. That's why you have to change your mind and come with me. Both of you. Please, SJ. Can't you see it's the only solution?'

Sarah looked at him in despair.

'Oh, Jamie, I wish I could. But I just can't. Can't you see what you are asking me is impossible? I understand about the boy. Really I do. And I do understand why you need to go back to see him and make sure he's all right.' Opening the door to her flat, she moved past him.

'It's up to you, Jamie. You have to choose. But it sounds to me as if you have made up your mind. And what's worse, if you stay I'll always feel guilty for forcing your hand. I don't want you to come to resent me for making you do something you didn't want to.'

'Why can't you trust me? What can't you trust the feelings we have for one another? Come with me. Please.' Jamie reached out and took Sarah by the arms. She could feel his fingers biting into her flesh. She looked at him, until at last he dropped his hands to his sides.

'That's always going to be the problem between us,' she said sadly, moving away from him. 'I don't trust you. Not as far as loving me is concerned, and maybe not as far as Calum is concerned. Once trust is broken, that's what happens. I realise that now. It's too late. Without that trust, there can never be a future for us.'

Jamie caught her by the arm. 'I won't accept that. I'm not going to allow you to throw away our chance for happiness. And you can't tell me that back there in the hotel meant nothing to you.'

'I'm only human, Jamie, as you're finding out. And there's a big difference between love and sex.'

'I don't believe you,' Jamie ground out between clenched teeth.

'Right now I don't care whether you believe me or not. And I'm too tired to discuss this right now. Accept it, Jamie. It's over between us. We can be friends and colleagues—after all, we will always share Calum—but we will never be anything more.'

Jamie dropped his hand, his mouth set in a stubborn line.

'OK, I'll go, but you and I will talk about this,' he said firmly. 'I'm not going to give up. Tomorrow evening when I get back from my climb. We are going to go somewhere where we can be alone and uninterrupted. I'll pick you up around seven.' And before Sarah had a chance to protest he had disappeared back into the night.

The next day, Sarah thought that Calum still felt a little warm and her usually placid baby was fractious and out of sorts.

'Perhaps I shouldn't have taken him to the wedding,' Sarah said to her mother.

'He's probably just teething,' her mother replied reassuringly.

'Perhaps,' Sarah said thoughtfully, 'but I'm just going to check his temperature anyway.'

Sarah took his temperature with a child thermometer. It was slightly raised, but not enough to cause concern. Maybe it was just teething or a mild bug. Somehow it was different when it was your own child. It was difficult to be objective. Much easier to tell whether it was something serious when it was somebody else's baby.

She decided to keep him indoors instead of the walk she had planned.

But as the day wore on, Calum became increasingly irritable. He didn't seem interested in his bottle and spent most of the day dozing in his mother's arms. It's just a mild bug, Sarah tried to reassure herself. If only she could ask Jamie. Not because he was Calum's father but because she trusted him as a doctor, despite everything.

Finally, mid-afternoon, she tried Jamie's mobile. The message came back that the caller was unavailable. He was probably up a mountain where the signal couldn't reach. Why was the man never around when she needed him? Instead, she sent him a text, asking him to call her when he returned home. If he was planning to pick her up at seven, he had obviously intended to be home before then.

But by six-thirty Jamie still hadn't called. Looking at Calum, she made a decision. Something was definitely wrong with her child. She phoned the hospital and asked them to page Dr Carty, the senior paediatrician at the hospital, and request that he call her at home.

She had met him when he had attended the department for a specialist paediatric opinion. She had found him thorough and caring and had trusted his opinion implicitly. When Dr Carty returned her call a few minutes later, she explained Calum's symptoms, trying to keep her voice calm and factual.

'I think we should see him at the hospital straight away. Can you bring him or would you like me to send an ambulance?'

Sarah was panic-stricken at his words. Had she waited too long? Had she put her child's health at risk? Dr Carty obviously thought that there could be a serious problem.

'I'm only a short distance away. I'll take him in my car. I can be there in ten minutes.'

'I'll meet you in A and E,' was the brisk reply.

Sarah bundled Calum into his outdoor suit. On her way out she stopped at her mother's to tell her that she was taking Calum to the hospital. Jean had just come out of the shower and was still in her dressing-gown.

'If you give me a minute, I'll get dressed and come with you.'

'I can't wait, Mum. Follow me when you're ready,' Sarah flung over her shoulder, already heading for the car.

Calum had stopped crying and had gone eerily quiet. As Sarah strapped him into his car seat, she knew for certain that there was something seriously wrong with her baby. She forced back tears of fear. It wouldn't do her child any good if she were to panic. For his sake, she needed to keep calm and think rationally.

As she was getting into the driver's seat, Jamie appeared at the window.

'Running away? Is the thought of dinner with me really that bad?' he said, a smile curling his mouth. Then he peered closer. 'Good God, Sarah, what is it?'

'It's Calum. He's sick. I'm taking him to A and E. Dr Carty's meeting us there.'

'Get in the back with Calum. You're in no state to drive,' Jamie said, taking control. Sarah knew it was useless to protest. Besides, now Jamie was there, all she felt was an overwhelming sense of relief.

As Jamie drove the short distance to the hospital, Sarah explained Calum's symptoms.

'It could be anything, Sarah,' he said, but she could tell from his grim voice that he, too, was thinking the same as her. Meningitis. Almost unable to look, Sarah pulled up Calum's outfit, searching for the tell-tale signs. She couldn't be sure in the dim light cast by the streetlights, but she thought she could just make out the faintest of rashes. She felt terror grip her.

'I think he's developing a rash, Jamie.' She could barely speak. Her jaw felt rigid with the effort of holding things together.

'Hold on, Sarah. Everything's going to be all

right.' But they both knew that if their diagnosis was correct, everything was far from all right.

Jamie drew up in front of the A and E entrance. He leapt out of the car tossing the keys to a porter who was outside, having a break. 'Park this somewhere,' he ordered, lifting Calum out of his seat.

There was something surreal about the evening, Sarah was thinking. Here she was back in her department, but instead of the usual familiarity it felt alien, frightening. Recognising Sarah and Jamie, one of the nursing staff, an experienced nurse called Mary, came over and held out her arms for Calum.

'Dr Carty told us to expect you. He's waiting in Resus. We'll take Calum through for you. If you'd just take a seat?'

Jamie ignored the nurses and strode towards Resus, Calum still in his arms and Sarah at his heels.

'You'd be better waiting outside,' Jamie said. 'I'll make sure he's OK.'

'I'm not leaving my son,' Sarah retorted. 'I know I can't be involved in his care, but I'm not letting him out of my sight.' She lifted her chin, praying that Jamie wouldn't argue with her. She simply didn't have the strength to fight him, too.

'Fine, but you stay in the background.' He turned to her, his dark eyes sombre. 'I promise you, Sarah, I won't let anything happen to our son.'

Jamie reluctantly handed over his son to Mary, who placed Calum's tiny body gently on a gurney. He was barely conscious and made no protest as Mary undressed his unresisting form.

Sarah reached for Jamie's hand and felt her fingernails dig into his palm. Jamie returned her squeeze reassuringly. 'He's in the best possible hands, SJ,' he said, but she could see the worry in his eyes.

Swiftly, one of the other nurses, who had introduced herself to the worried parents as Rosemary, attached the leads of the ECG monitor to Calum's small chest and a pulse oximeter to his finger.

'He's tachycardic,' Mary told Sarah, 'but at least his oxygen saturation is normal.'

It only took a couple of minutes for Dr Carty

to arrive and carry out a thorough examination, but to Sarah it seemed like an eternity. The paediatrician lifted Calum's head and Sarah knew that he, too, suspected meningitis. He shifted his attention to the rash covering the infant's body. To Sarah's frantic gaze it seemed as if the rash had become more prominent even since she had first noticed it in the car.

Dr Carty turned to Jamie and Sarah. 'I know you are worried that this might be meningitis, but we won't know until we have carried out more tests. We'll need to do a lumbar puncture, Paul,' he ordered the junior doctor, who had joined the group in Resus. 'Start IV antibiotics immediately. Could you also send off bloods for haematology, U and Es and do blood cultures? Mary, could you set up for an LP? And, Rosemary, could you get a urine specimen for culture?'

The next couple of hours passed in a haze. Sarah could hardly bear it as the paediatrician inserted the needle into the space between her son's vertebrae to draw fluid. It was such a small spine. Such a small space. What if the needle slipped? Although Sarah had carried out the same procedure a hundred times herself without incident, she knew that occasionally things did go wrong. It was the worst part of being a doctor, knowing what could go wrong. All the complications of meningitis—septicaemia, amputation, brain damage, death—whirled around her mind.

'He's a bit young for bacterial meningitis,' Jamie tried to reassure Sarah. 'And even if he does have it, many, many pull through and lead perfectly healthy lives. We have to stay positive.'

'We won't know whether he has meningitis, or which form until we get the results,' Dr Carty agreed. 'Let's keep our fingers crossed, but even if it is viral meningitis, he's still pretty poorly.'

Sarah felt utterly wretched. Why had she waited so long? She should have acted sooner.

Jamie was clearly reading her thoughts. 'You couldn't have known, SJ. Think. You know this illness comes on very rapidly. You brought him in as soon as you could.'

'He's started on IV antibiotics. I think we've

caught it in time. But we are going to have to admit him to the paediatric intensive care unit for observation. The next twenty-four hours will be critical,' Dr Carty informed Sarah. 'You know that there are lots of viral illnesses that can cause rashes, although I'm afraid it almost certainly is meningitis. But I won't be sure until we get the results of all his tests some time tomorrow.'

As Calum was being taken up to Intensive Care, Sarah turned to Jean, who had arrived while Calum had been in Resus. Seeing the stricken look on her mother's face, Sarah almost broke down.

'Could you go home and collect some stuff for me, please, Mum?' she said, tears close to the surface.

'Of course, darling,' her mother replied, clearly struggling to keep her own emotions under control. 'But I don't want to leave you on your own.'

Jamie stepped up, lines of worry evident on his face. 'Don't worry, Jean, she won't be. I'll stay with them both.'

'Go home, Jamie,' Sarah said wearily. 'I can

manage. Besides, one of us has to be fit to work tomorrow.'

'You can stop worrying about work. I'll see to everything. As for going home, not a chance—he's my son, too.'

Sarah looked at his face. She was surprised to see that how much he was also suffering. He was right. Whatever happened between them in the future, it would be too cruel to stop him being with his son when he so obviously needed to be.

She reached out for his hand and felt his strength flow from him to her. For now she needed him, too. Right now nothing else mattered.

The nurses in the intensive care ward had offered to make up a bed in the relatives' room for Sarah or Jamie should they wish to catnap.

'We've sedated Calum and he seems peaceful. Why don't you try and get some sleep?' they had suggested. But both Jamie and Sarah had refused. Sarah didn't want to leave her son for a moment in case he woke up and wanted her. Instead, they found a couple of armchairs and made themselves as comfortable as they could by the bedside without getting in the nurses' way.

The night wore on. Jamie and Sarah watched over their son as he lay in the cot. More than anything Sarah wanted to hold her son in her arms, but the leads and drips that fed him and monitored his condition prevented her from doing anything except stroke his face with her finger.

She was barely conscious of Jamie standing behind her, massaging her shoulders and stroking her hair, but she was glad of his presence.

'God, what's taking so long? Why haven't they brought us some news?' The words sounded as they had been ripped from Jamie's body. 'Sorry. I know these things take time. But not being able to do anything makes me think of my father. It reminds me of how helpless I felt then, too. What is the point of all our medical training if we can't help those we love?'

'At least your father loved you,' Sarah said quietly. 'Mine didn't seem to care whether I lived or died.' Memories of her father's betrayal came rushing back. 'He left Mum and me when

I was about Calum's age,' she went on, almost as if she was talking to herself. 'He came back to see me once or twice, but then his visits fizzled out and I never saw him again.' As always, the memory of sitting waiting for a father who had never come caused her almost unbearable pain. She was determined her son would never suffer the same feelings of abandonment and rejection.

'I'm sorry, SJ, I didn't know about your father. You never told me.'

'It turns out there was quite a lot we never told one another,' Sarah replied with a small smile. 'I guess somehow we were too wrapped up in just being together to ever really talk. I always thought there would be plenty of time for us to really get to know one another.'

The time they had been together had been spent in a flurry of activity. There had never seemed to be a right time to tell him about her father.

'And then I left,' Jamie said flatly.

'Yes. I thought you were different. I never believed that you would do to me what my father did to my mother. Against my better judgement, I allowed myself to trust you and what we had.'

'I had my reasons,' Jamie reminded her. 'I know now I was wrong, but I did what I did to protect you. I knew I was falling in love with you, and I guess I panicked.' He turned her towards him. 'You have to believe me when I tell you that I will never abandon my child.'

'What if there's no choice?' Sarah's voice broke. 'What if we lose him, Jamie? I couldn't bear it.'

'Sarah, listen to me,' Jamie said urgently. 'That is not going to happen. I won't let it.'

In the early hours of the morning Dr Carty came in to see them.

Sarah held her breath as she waited for him to bring them up to date.

'The initial results are back. It is meningitis, but it looks like it's most likely to be the viral strain. We'll know for sure when we get the rest of the results later in the day.' When she heard the news, Sarah was powerless to stop the tears. Although it was a less deadly strain than bacterial meningitis, Sarah knew that Calum was far from out of the woods. They couldn't be sure he'd recover. Not yet.

Oblivious of the staff around them, Jamie pulled her into his arms and held her as sobs racked her body. 'Shh.' He stroked her hair. 'It's going to be all right, I promise you.'

Sarah looked into his eyes. He returned the look, his eyes grim, but whatever she saw there calmed her.

For the rest of the long night, Jamie and Sarah sat in silence, each preoccupied with their own thoughts. Neither could bring themselves to discuss what could happen to Calum. Every now and then Jamie would get up and fetch them both a coffee from the vending machine. Nurses recorded Calum's vital signs at regular intervals. 'He seems to be holding his own,' they kept reassuring the worried parents. 'And so far there doesn't seem to be any signs that he's developed septicaemia.' Sarah shuddered at the thought of her tiny son battling the deadly blood infection. But if Calum survived, it would be the next big worry. With septicaemia there was always the possibility that amputation would be required. Sarah pushed the negative thoughts to the back of her mind. *Calum was going to be all right—he had to be!*

As dawn was breaking, Jamie left the ward. 'I'll be back as soon as I can,' he whispered. 'Any change—even the slightest—get the ward to page me.'

Calum was still sleeping when Jamie arrived back a couple of hours later. He had changed into theatre greens and had shaved, but he still looked tired and drawn. Sarah couldn't remember ever seeing him look so vulnerable.

'I've arranged for the locum who was covering at the weekend to stay on and cover nights. I'll manage the day shift on my own. The ward can easily page me here if I'm needed. In the meantime, management is trying to find us some extra cover.'

Sarah simply nodded. She couldn't bring herself to care. All that mattered was her son.

As the hours wore on staff from the all over the hospital popped their heads in, asking about Calum, how he was, was there anything they could do? Although Sarah appreciated their concern, anything that took her attention away from Calum was a distraction she didn't need.

Jamie was there most of the time, occasionally leaving the room to answer the phone or go to the ward. Jean had come and gone. Sarah had insisted she get some rest. Her mother couldn't survive on no sleep. Sarah was used to it and while Calum's life was still in danger, she couldn't bear to close her eyes for a moment.

By late afternoon the next day, Calum's condition was beginning to improve. 'He's responding well to treatment and you picked it up so quickly that, although it's early days yet, I think he's going to make a full recovery. He's a tough little mite. Takes after his mother, obviously.' Dr Carty smiled at Sarah's relief. 'We're going to start reducing the sedation. He should wake up soon.'

Again Sarah broke down in tears. But this time, as she found comfort in Jamie's arms once more, her tears were of relief. Calum had survived the first twenty-four hours without developing septicaemia. This was the news they had prayed for.

'Thank God,' Jamie whispered into her hair. His voice shook with suppressed emotion. Clearly the last hours had taken their toll on him too.

Although still poorly, Sarah knew that her baby was well on his way to recovery. She pulled free of Jamie's arms and made a feeble attempt to smooth her ruffled hair.

'The department's quiet just now, SJ. Why don't you go home and try and catch a couple of hours' sleep? You look exhausted.'

'You don't look so hot yourself,' Sarah teased wearily. But she felt a pang of sympathy for him. The lines around his eyes and brows seemed to have deepened overnight, and his eyes looked even darker with fatigue. After all, he had been running the department in between spending every spare moment at Calum's bedside.

'I'm all right. I'm more used to staying up all night than most. But you need to get some rest.'

'I'll have a shower in the department and maybe snatch a couple of hours in the side ward,' Sarah compromised. 'I'll come and relieve you after that. But—'

'I know, I know. If there's any change, I'll call you immediately. Now, shoo, woman, before I carry you out of here.' Seeing Jamie taking a step towards her as if he had every intention of carrying out his threat, Sarah beat a hasty retreat.

When she returned a couple of hours, later feeling a whole lot better for her shower and nap, she found Jamie asleep with a sleeping Calum in his arms. As she looked at the two figures she felt her heart twist. Whatever she tried to tell herself, these were the two most important people in her world. She shivered at the thought that she had almost lost one permanently and would never truly have the other. As if conscious of her scrutiny, Jamie's eyes flickered open.

'Hi, there,' he said softly. 'Feeling better?'

'Much,' she said, her throat tight with emotion. 'Why don't I take over here and you get some rest?'

'Perhaps in a little while,' Jamie stalled.

Sarah sat down in the chair beside Jamie and Calum. Her son seemed so settled in his father's embrace. She reached over and tenderly stroked his fine baby hair.

'I'm going to miss him so much. The thought of being on the other side of the world from him doesn't bear thinking about,' Jamie said hoarsely.

Sarah felt tears well up as she watched him gaze, mesmerised, at his sleeping child.

'Then stay,' she said quietly

'Don't you know that's what I want to do more than anything else in this world? But I have to go back. See Sibongele, work at the hospital at least until they find someone to replace me.'

'And then? Will you come back?'

'You leave me no choice, SJ.' He looked down at his sleeping child. 'I don't want him to grow up not knowing his father.'

'What about the hospital in Africa? Won't you miss it? Won't they miss you?'

For a moment she could see the sadness that clouded Jamie's eyes.

'Yes,' he said heavily. 'I'll miss them and I know they will miss having an experienced doctor around. But…' He hesitated, as if unsure whether to go on. 'But it's not just the work and the feeling that I'm letting the hospital down.

It's Sibongele. I feel as if I'm letting him down, too. I don't know how he'll feel when I tell him I'm leaving. I just know he's going to think I've abandoned him as well.' Jamie stood up with his son in his arms and strode towards the window. He looked out without saying anything.

'But,' he continued, his back still facing her, 'if you and Calum won't come back with me, and it's the only way to be with you both, then I have no choice.' He turned and smiled briefly at her, as if to reassure her he felt no bitterness towards her.

He must love Calum, Sarah thought, if he was prepared to make such a sacrifice to be with his child. But where did that leave her? Why couldn't she believe that he cared for her? But how could she when he was prepared to leave them both? Surely, if he meant what he said, if he *really* cared about her and Calum, he would put them first—no matter how he felt about his responsibilities in Africa. And perhaps if he had, she would have started to believe in him again. But this way, his insistence that he had to go back made her think that he only truly cared about those he had left in Africa, and his son, of course. She had no doubts that he loved his son and wanted to be with him. Her head was beginning to ache from asking herself questions that didn't appear to have any answers.

'When will you go?'

'I've provisionally booked my flight for next Monday. They expect to discharge Calum home in a day or two and I want to make absolutely sure he's well before I go. That will give you the rest of the week off to be at home with him.'

'And when will you be back?' Suddenly Sarah couldn't bear the thought of not seeing him every day.

'Why? Will you miss me?' he teased, a wicked glint in his brown eyes. 'I'll be back as soon as I can, but it may some time—several weeks, even a few months.'

A few months? Sarah was aghast. She had been thinking a couple of weeks, three at the most.

'Calum will miss you. And, besides, we'll be a doctor down before you come back.' Sarah wasn't prepared to admit just how much she was going to miss him.

'I know. I'm sorry about that. But the other locum will continue to cover while I'm away. And the interviews for the third post are next week. Apparently they've got a couple of outstanding candidates lined up who are ready to start straight away.'

Sarah couldn't tell him that she didn't care how outstanding the potential appointees were, it was Jamie she wanted working beside her. More than just working beside her.

'I'll be back for a visit in two, maximum three weeks. I don't want to be away from this little lad any longer than I have to. I've missed enough of his life already and if I have my way, once I return for good, he and I will have a lot of catching up to do.' He looked at Sarah, his dark eyes serious. 'And you and I have some unfinished business, too.'

As Jamie had predicted, Calum was pronounced fit and healthy and discharged home a couple of days later. Jamie was a frequent visitor to the flat in the days leading up to his departure for Africa, but Sarah rarely found herself alone with him. And when she did, he talked about work, keeping her informed about the department, the type of cases they had been dealing with and gossip about the staff.

They had appointed the new consultant. Sarah had left Calum with her mother and attended the interviews. Two of the three candidates had been a husband-and-wife team who were on a two-year working visa from Australia. They had been keen to get jobs in the same hospital. The wife, a pretty woman with an outgoing manner, had indicated that she would prefer part-time hours in the future, if possible, as they were trying for their first child. 'And I'd love to be at home at least for the first year or two.' she had confided to Sarah.

At her words a germ of an idea was beginning to form in Sarah's mind. Calum's illness had shaken her badly. Part of her still felt guilty, although she knew there was nothing more she could have done to prevent Calum becoming unwell. Perhaps she could reduce her hours and do a job share? Spend more time being a mother yet still have a career? She made up her mind to give the thought some serious consideration before discussing it with the personnel department. The hospital had appointed the husband, and the wife had another interview lined up at one of the smaller hospitals on the outskirts of the city in a couple of weeks' time, so she'd have to make a decision soon.

Shortly before Jamie left for Africa, Lizzie returned from honeymoon. She was horrified and sympathetic to learn about Calum's illness.

'Poor you,' she sympathised. 'You must have got a terrible fright.'

Sarah could feel a lump come to her throat at the memory.

'I really thought I was going to lose him, Lizzie,' she confided, a break in her voice.

'But you didn't,' Lizzie said firmly. 'I heard that Jamie was distraught. Obviously everyone knows now.'

'Funny how little it matters. It probably caused some gossip at the time, but everyone was fantastic, really concerned and offering help any chance they got.'

'And you and Jamie?' Lizzie's hazel eyes were lit up with curiosity. 'I gather he's thinking of applying for a permanent consultant post. The staff are over the moon. Absolutely delighted that he's planning to be a permanent feature in the department. And,' she added impishly, 'there is probably more than one who is working out how they can become a permanent feature in his life. Although I suspect that slot is already taken.' She arched an eye brow at Sarah, making her meaning clear.

Sarah chewed her lip. 'He's going back to Africa and it could be some time before he returns…if he ever does come back.' She swallowed hard against the lump that had formed in her throat. 'And there is no Jamie and me. There never will be. Oh, I think Jamie *will* be back…to see his son, if for no other reason. But how long for?' She shook her head sadly. 'I can't deny Calum his father, just because we couldn't work things out. I know only too well the heartache of not knowing your own dad…' Sarah trailed off.

So that's the way the land lay, thought Lizzie, but she was wise enough to keep her own counsel. From what she had gathered from the nursing staff, Jamie was besotted not only with his son but the son's very beautiful mother. Was Sarah the only one in the department who didn't know how Jamie felt?

CHAPTER NINE

'OF COURSE I can't go. How can you possibly manage without me?' Jean said.

'I'll try and change my weekend on call,' said Sarah. 'Although I've already had so much time off.' Sarah let her words tail off. Since Calum had been discharged from hospital she had been at home with him. But now that he had made a full recovery, she needed to get back to work and share some of the load. She knew from Lizzie that every moment that Jamie hadn't being spending with Calum had been spent in the department, picking up the extra work that her enforced absence had left. Sarah's mother had won a weekend break at an exclusive new health spa that had opened just south of the border. It was a once-in-a-lifetime opportunity and sharing the worry of Calum's illness had tired her mother. She deserved—no, needed—some time off to relax.

When the phone rang she picked it up, still thinking of what to do.

'Oh, hello, Jamie,' she said, recognising his deep voice immediately. 'Calum's fine. He's just about to have his lunch.' Jamie phoned regularly to check up on his son.

'What's up? Are you sure Calum's fine?' he asked, as usual immediately picking up when something was bothering her.

'Honestly, he's perfectly all right. It's just…' She hesitated, then decided to share her problem After all, it did concern him, too, both as Calum's father and as a fellow colleague. 'Mum's had this opportunity to go on a weekend break to a spa, but I'm supposed to be on call this weekend. Normally she'd move into my flat so she can be here for Calum if I'm called out. She's said she won't go but I really think she should,' she said, ignoring her mother's frantic gestures.

'Of course she should go.' Jamie agreed at once. 'I'll do your weekend on call. It's no problem.'

'I really don't want to take more time off work. Besides, you've done more than your fair share of being on call. You're not superhuman, Jamie.' Although, as she said this, she wondered if he was. Over the last week it had definitely seemed as if Jamie was superhuman. Heaven only knew when he had found the time to sleep. Slowly an idea was beginning to formulate in her mind.

'Unless…' she said slowly.

'Unless?' Jamie prompted.

'Unless you move in here for the weekend. You could look after Calum if I get called out. You can have the spare bedroom. It'll give you a chance to spend some time with your son before you leave, and an opportunity to get a break from work.'

There was a brief silence at the other end of the phone.

'Perhaps you don't think you are up to it? After all, a young baby can be hard work,' she added.

'Of course I can manage,' Jamie said briskly. 'How hard can it be? If that's what you'd rather do, SJ, it's no problem. I'll bring some stuff over tonight. You can take me through his routine and I can be there when you go to work in the morning.'

As she put down the phone, Sarah felt a small smile tugging at the corner of her mouth. She rather thought that Jamie Campbell was going to get a bit of a shock. She ignored the little tingle of pleasure that accompanied the thought of Jamie being in her flat for the weekend. She was doing this for Calum, she told herself firmly. Father and son needed some time together before Jamie went away. As for her, it was nothing to do with storing up memories for the future—it was simply that she and Jamie needed to stay on friendly terms, for Calum's sake. She turned to her mother who was looking at her enquiringly.

'That's settled, Mum. You can go for your weekend. You'll have gathered that Jamie is going to come and stay while you're away.'

Sarah's mother looked thoughtful. 'Are you sure he can manage?'

'He'll have to. If he wants to be a father to Calum, he's going to have to learn how.'

* * *

The next morning, as Sarah closed the door behind her, Jamie looked at his son. Calum was sitting in his high chair, waving his spoon around. Drops of what Jamie could only think of as gunk was flying from the spoon, spreading around the kitchen.

'Hey,' he said in surprise as a splodge landed on his face. 'Good aim.' Maybe Calum was destined to be a cricket player rather than a climber with that kind of throwing technique. But how had he managed to get so much in his hair? And all over his night things?

Sarah had left Jamie a list of instructions, starting with feeding Calum his breakfast, followed by a bath, getting him dressed and then a trip to the supermarket to pick up some nappies.

As Jamie took in the chaos around him, he was beginning to get the feeling that this wasn't going to be such a piece of cake after all. Still, he had a point to prove to Sarah. And surely a man of his resourcefulness could get through the next few hours without disaster?

Two hours later, he had finally bathed and dressed Calum. That wasn't too difficult, he thought smugly. There only remained the problem of how to get himself showered. He couldn't go anywhere, not even to the supermarket, until he had cleaned off the encrusted food that seemed to cling to every part of his head. Finally he had the answer. He strapped a protesting Calum into his high chair and lifted the chair with Calum into it and set it down in front of the shower. Calum clearly thought the novel situation deserved his full attention and watched quietly as Jamie took his shower. Jamie decided against shaving. He still had the shopping to do.

Sarah and Jamie had swapped cars for the day. Jamie was just about to turn the key in the ignition when he paused. Something was missing. What had he forgotten? Calum! With a mumbled curse he shot out of the car, taking the steps to Sarah's front door two at a time. He had left Calum in the house! Luckily his son was still mesmerised by the activity bar on his cot and hadn't noticed his father's two-minute absence. The workings of the car seat was another challenge, but eventually the infant was strapped in and Jamie could set off for the shops. Hell, that was a close call, he thought as he pulled up in the car park. What on earth would Sarah have thought had he actually left without Calum? She wouldn't trust him ever again.

As Jamie shopped with Calum in the cart— it had taken him several goes until an assistant had taken pity on him and shown him which cart to use and how to place Calum in it—one or two of the female customers came up to them and, under the pretext of admiring the child, attempted to flirt with Jamie. One even went as far to ask him out. 'Sorry, I'm committed,' he told her. And as he said the words they felt good. He *was* committed to Sarah. Whatever she felt about him, he was still determined to be part of her life.

It was after six in the evening by the time Sarah arrived back from work. Jamie felt pleased with himself. He had bought the nappies and hadn't forgotten to bring Calum back with him. He had played with him and they had both managed a nap after lunch. Calum had cried when Jamie had tried to put him in his cot for his sleep so Jamie had simply stretched out on the sofa with Calum wrapped in his arms, and that had seemed to work perfectly well. The nappy-changing hadn't been an unmitigated success, he had to admit. He couldn't quite seem to get the sticky bits to go where they should but he had managed to get the nappies to stay on after a fashion and Calum hadn't seem to mind that they hadn't fitted terribly snugly. He had fed him his evening meal—a mashed-up concoction of red and white that Sarah had left—so altogether he was feeling pretty pleased with the way the day had gone.

However, when he saw the expression in Sarah's eyes as she took in the chaos that surrounded her, he realised that she wasn't entirely of the same opinion.

'What on earth happened here?' she gasped, as she removed her coat and held out her arms for her son.

Jamie followed her gaze. Food debris littered the kitchen table. Calum's clothes were scattered around the usually immaculate sitting room. He had meant to tidy up a little before she returned, but somehow he hadn't seemed to find the time. How on earth did she do it?

'I didn't notice till now,' he said with a sheepish smile, peeling himself out of the chair he'd slumped into. 'You relax there for a moment while I tidy up a bit.'

Sarah smiled. 'Don't worry, it can wait. I'm sorry I was back so late. We had a few difficult cases. Stuff that I couldn't leave. I didn't even manage lunch. That reminds me,' she said with a mischievous look at Jamie, 'what's for supper?'

Jamie hit his head with his hand. 'Supper,' he groaned, 'I'd completely forgotten. How on earth do you find the time to cook, as well as everything else?'

'Practice. But there have been days…' She let the words hang in the air.

'Right,' Jamie said, 'I'll cook, or at least order us a take-away. I think there is enough mayhem in here without adding to it. What do you fancy? Pizza? Chinese?'

'Chinese will be lovely. There's a great take-away just a short walk away. Why don't you go down and get us something while I sort things out here?'

Jamie knew better than to argue. Besides, he could do with a walk in the fresh air. By the time he returned, Sarah had restored the flat to some kind of order and Calum was ready for bed. She put him on the floor while they ate. He was just beginning to make crawling movements and they watched his attempts, fascinated.

'He'll be walking before long,' Jamie said proudly.

'In a couple of months perhaps,' Sarah said, amused. 'Gosh, I'm tired. I think I'll have a long bath once Calum goes down and then have an early night. I hope it's quiet tonight.'

'Anyone in at the moment causing concern? 'Jamie asked, and they chatted about work while Calum had his last bottle of the day.

When Sarah returned from putting Calum in his cot, Jamie had started running a bath for her. He lit a fire while she soaked and put some soft music on the stereo. He hoped the evening would provide an opportunity for him to begin wooing Sarah in earnest. And as he thought of her lying in the bath, images of her naked body filled his thoughts. But as much as he wanted her, he was determined to take it slowly. He had to convince her that his feelings were sincere.

When she eventually appeared from the bathroom with her hair wrapped up in a towel, her bathrobe pulled around her and her cheeks flushed from the heat, he almost forgot his resolve. It was all he could do to stop from striding over to her, picking her up and carrying her over to the bed.

'Would you like some coffee before bed?' he said instead.

'Not coffee. I've had too much as it is. But a hot chocolate would be lovely.'

By the time Jamie returned with the hot drink Sarah had fallen asleep on the sofa, her long legs curled up and tucked under her. Just as well, Jamie thought as he fetched a blanket from the spare room to put over her. He didn't know if he really did have the strength to resist her.

When Sarah woke up the next morning she felt a little disoriented. The last she remembered was sitting in front of the fire while she waited for Jamie to bring her the hot chocolate she had requested. But here she was in her own bed. Her cheeks flamed as she realised that Jamie must have carried her. She hadn't been wearing anything under her bathrobe and now she was completely naked under the covers.

She followed the smell of coffee into the kitchen, where Jamie was feeding a laughing Calum his breakfast. He was only wearing a pair of jeans low on his hips and his muscular chest was bare. His hair was still damp from his shower and he smelt of soap and shaving cream. He had nicked himself while shaving and she suppressed the impulse to reach out and touch his face. She averted her eyes hoping that by doing so she could banish the effect his half-naked body was having on her.

'After yesterday I thought it would be a good idea to have my shower before this little fellow woke up. Unfortunately I didn't have time to finish getting dressed when I heard him stirring.'

'Good grief. What time is it?' She glanced at her watch and was horrified to find it was almost nine. 'I should have been at work half an hour ago. Why didn't you wake me?' she accused Jamie, stopping just long enough to grab the coffee-cup out of his hand and to plant several kisses on Calum's upturned face, before heading back to the bedroom.

'Hey, no need to rush,' Jamie called after her. 'You needed to sleep. I phoned the department an hour ago, and everything's under control. You can take your time.'

Sarah didn't know whether to be grateful to Jamie or furious with him. He had to realise that he couldn't make decisions for her. Even though he was trying to help, it wasn't up to him to decide when she should go into work. But, she admitted to herself, perhaps the real reason for her feelings of discomfort was caused by having Jamie in such close proximity. She was glad he was spending time with Calum, but having him so near, sharing the flat, was doing her own resolve to keep him at a distance no good at all. Thank goodness her mother was returning that evening and Jamie would be going back to his own place. She didn't know if she could keep her hormones under control for very much longer.

When Sarah arrived back that evening she found a completely different scenario to the one of the day before. The flat was spotless and Calum was dressed in his nightwear. The fire had been lit and delicious smells of a lamb curry were floating from the kitchen. Jamie was stirring a pot as he balanced Calum in his spare arm. Both males were looking into the pot with great interest. Calum was babbling away as if discussing the ingredients with his father.

What on earth happened here? Sarah thought immediately suspicious, shrugging off her coat. Had her mother returned early and been drafted in to help? That would be cheating. Jamie had to learn to cope on his own.

'Is my mother back?' she asked.

'Jean? Yes, she returned a short while ago. Popped in to say hello and that she'll come to see you later,' Jamie replied, handing Calum over to Sarah. 'Here, you take Calum while I take your coat and fix you a drink. You *are* finished for the evening?'

'Yes, Dr Holden has taken over. A small white wine would be lovely. If there is any?'

'There's white and red actually.'

'Have you been shopping as well as all this?' Sarah couldn't believe what she was seeing. 'Has my mother been helping?'

'Of course not.' Jamie hesitated for a moment. 'Actually, I phoned up an agency and arranged for someone to come over for a couple of hours to do some housework and shopping,' he admitted. 'Cost me an arm and a leg, what with it being Sunday and short notice, but I just don't see how it would have been possible otherwise.'

Sarah had to laugh. 'I do think that's cheating, Jamie, but what the heck—it's your money.'

'I'm sure I'll get better with practice,' he said, handing her a chilled glass of Chablis, 'but at the moment I'll take all the help I can get. Your mother did suggest she take Calum over to her for the night. She says she's missed him and would really like some time with him on her own. Do you mind?'

Sarah didn't know if she minded or not. On the one hand she hadn't seen her son for the best part of the day, on the other an occasional night off wouldn't do either of them any harm.

'Is she coming for supper?' Sarah asked. 'What is it anyway? Did you cook that yourself or has it been sent over from a deli that does outside catering?'

'I'm not completely hopeless!' Jamie protested. 'I was hoping that this needn't be for tonight, but could go in the freezer for another time. Actually, I have also taken the liberty of booking us a table at a restaurant in town.' He named a place that Sarah had heard about and had been dying to try. 'Unless you're too tired to go out?'

Making her mind up, Sarah smiled up at Jamie. 'I'd love to go out for something to eat.' She didn't tell him that she didn't know whether she could trust herself alone with him in the flat. Not without the limiting presence of Calum. Besides since the night of the wedding she hadn't left the house, apart from trips to the supermarket and the hospital. A change of scenery was needed, and time with Jamie on neutral ground would be safest.

Sarah's mother arrived a little later and, after bringing Sarah up to date with the news of her weekend, took a sleepy Calum back with her to her flat.

Jamie returned to his hospital digs to have a shave and change, while Sarah had a quick shower and applied some make-up. She knew the restaurant was quite formal and had slipped on a simple black knee-length dress that she thought would be sufficiently formal without going overboard. She twisted her hair into a French plait that emphasised the fine features of her face, and added her favourite green earrings and high heels. When the doorbell rang, signalling Jamie's return, she opened the door to his admiring wolf whistle.

Sarah resisted the impulse to wolf whistle back. He looked jaw-droppingly gorgeous, she thought. He was wearing a dark, well-tailored suit, which emphasised his lean frame, with a shirt in the palest pink and a navy tie. He looked incredibly handsome and suave. Sarah felt her heart turn over.

'You look amazing,' he said softly, his eyes gleaming. 'Are you sure you still want to go out?'

Sarah chose to ignore the meaning in his words and the look in his eyes. 'Let's go,' she said quickly.

Jamie opened the door of his sports car and Sarah sank into the soft leather seats. The car smelt of the leather and the faint tang of after-shave. Like Jamie, it was very masculine.

Jamie drove quickly and expertly and it was barely twenty minutes before they were being seated by the maître d'. Sarah took in the plush surroundings. The floor-to-ceiling windows looked over the city, its lights a diamanté bracelet of twinkling colour. The tables were laid with crisp white tablecloths and silver knives and forks. Candles cast a soft light. The restaurant was filled to capacity and the soft murmur of the other diners filled the air. Delicious smells drifted in from the kitchen. Suddenly Sarah was starving.

Jamie was an attentive and amusing dinner companion. They kept to neutral subjects, mainly about the work they shared. Jamie spoke about his work in Africa and as he spoke about the hospital, telling Sarah about the types of cases they dealt with, how children still died from malnutrition and mothers in childbirth, Sarah began to appreciate the depth of his passion for his work. He told her about Sibongele, the orphan who'd had been in the children's ward for several months. He spoke again of how the boy had developed a strong attachment to him.

'And I've grown fond of him, too. He's very bright and the mission school has offered him a scholarship. One day, with luck and hard work, he'll be working at the hospital as a doctor. All he needs right now is a little stability in his life.'

'You miss it all, don't you?' said Sarah

'Yes.' For a moment there was a far-away look in Jamie's eyes. 'It's such a beautiful country—and the people. They really appreciate the smallest thing you can do for them. It's just frustrating not to be able to do more.'

'You must be keen to get back,' Sarah prompted

'Yes, I am, although I'll miss you and Calum.

Still, it won't be for ever. Anyway, let's talk about something more cheerful.'

The rest of the evening passed quickly. Jamie told her more about the places he had visited in Africa and some stories that had her laughing out loud. She couldn't remember the last time she had enjoyed herself so much. She was so busy listening to Jamie she was unaware of the waiter topping up her glass. It wasn't until they stood up that she realised the wine she had drunk had made her head swim. It had been so long since she had drunk more than a glass of wine that the extra glass or two was having the strangest effect on her. Jamie, on the other hand, had kept to mineral water as he was driving.

She was still feeling a little light-headed by the time they pulled up outside her flat. She chose to believe it was the extra alcohol that was giving her the warm glow rather than Jamie's company.

'Would you like to come up for a coffee?' she asked Jamie, not wanting the evening to come to an end just yet.

Jamie looked at her speculatively. 'Just for a moment. Just to make sure you get in OK.'

Sarah felt herself bristle. He was doing it again. Treating her as if she were some helpless female who needed looking after.

'I am perfectly able to see myself in,' she replied tartly

'Nevertheless, I'll come up for a moment.' As Sarah eased herself out of the low-slung sports car, she stumbled slightly in her high heels.

'Bloody shoes.' She grimaced, hoping she hadn't twisted her ankle.

'Come on.' Jamie laughed, getting out of the car and going to her side. 'I could always carry you up the stairs.'

'You put a hand on me, Jamie Campbell, and I'll…'

But before she could finish her threat, Jamie was advancing towards her, a wicked glint in his eyes. 'You know I never could resist a challenge,' he said, picking her up and throwing her over his shoulder in a fireman's lift. Ignoring Sarah's beating fists, he carried her up the short flight of steps to the front door. He took the key that Sarah had given him in case of emergencies from his pocket and opened the door. Still ignoring her cries and threats, he deposited her gently on the sofa.

Sarah looked at him, eyes blazing, 'You, you Neanderthal, you!' she spat finally.

'I was only trying to help a damsel in distress!' Jamie replied, grinning broadly.

'I'm more distressed now! You could have picked me up in a more elegant fashion!' Sarah retorted, before seeing the funny side and beginning to laugh. 'Not exactly a bride being carried over the threshold, was it?' As soon as the words were out, she could have bitten her tongue.

'I mean,' she added hastily 'not really romantic.' Oh, dear, she thought, this was going from bad to worse.

'If it's romance you want…' Jamie said, pulling her up gently by her arms before finding her lips. He held her in his arms while he dropped kisses light as raindrops on her hair. Sarah took a deep breath. She knew she should pull away, but she couldn't quite bring herself to remove herself from the comfort of his arms. Just a few more minutes, she thought. He's going to be away for a while.

Jamie groaned before finding her mouth. His kisses sent sparks of desire through her body. She knew if she didn't stop him soon, she would never be able to stop. And this wasn't what she needed.

With an almost unbearable effort she pulled herself out of his embrace and stepped back. She couldn't think coherently when she was in his arms. She needed space.

'No, Jamie,' she said, her voice tinged with regret. 'I am not going to sleep with you again—however much I want to,' she admitted. 'Good sex—OK, fantastic sex,' she conceded when he cocked his eyebrow at her, 'just isn't enough for me.'

Jamie dropped his hands to his sides. He looked at her, his brown eyes serious.

'Do you think that's all I want from you? Sex? Good God, woman, don't you know me better than that?'

'What is it you want from me, Jamie?'

'I want to be with you. Share your life. Go to sleep with you. Wake up in the morning with you. I want us to bring up our son together.

Don't you know that I love you?' The last words were ground out as if ripped from his body. 'I never thought I'd ever say that to a woman. But I'm saying it now.'

For a long moment Sarah let his words sing through her body. How long had she waited to hear him say those words? But now it was too late. She still couldn't bring herself to trust him. He wanted Calum. There was no doubt in her mind about that. But she couldn't shake the thought that he would tell her he loved her, marry her even, do and say anything to achieve his own ends—to have Calum in Africa with him. She didn't doubt that he found her attractive, wanted her sexually, enough to marry her and have her with him, but lust and a need to be with his son wasn't enough for her.

'I wish I could believe you, Jamie,' she said sadly. 'But you've hurt me too much. I just can't trust you to be honest with me. You left me once. I couldn't bear for that to happen again.'

'God dammit, SJ. I've promised to come back. What else can I do to prove that I love you?'

'You're still leaving me now.'

'But only for a short while. You know I have to go back right now. But I've told you I am prepared to give it all up for you and Calum as soon as I have honoured my responsibilities. Isn't that enough?'

'And how will I know that you won't eventually resent me for that? That eventually you'll feel trapped. Come to hate me. And leave again. It's not just me. I have to think about my son.'

'*Our* son, Sarah,' Jamie reminded her. He looked at her calmly. 'OK, you win for now, but when I come back I'm going to do whatever it takes to convince you that you and I belong together. You can't hold out on me for ever. I won't let you. That's one thing you can count on.' He kissed her lightly on the lips. 'Look after yourself and our child until I get back.'

When he had gone Sarah stood for a while. Thoughts rushed through her mind. He had said he loved her, wanted to spend his life with her. What was wrong with her that she couldn't believe him when every nerve in her body was straining towards him? And how was she going to live without him?

CHAPTER TEN

SARAH missed Jamie in the weeks that he was away. Dr Shepherd was an excellent colleague, but Sarah had to admit it just wasn't the same as having Jamie around.

He phoned a few times to enquire after Calum, but he had warned Sarah that getting access to international calls was difficult with the rather antiquated phone system that the hospital used. He sounded exhilarated when he spoke briefly about his work at the hospital. The way he described it made Sarah want to see the place for herself.

She knew that Jamie was due back for a short visit at the weekend, but he was unsure how soon he'd be able to catch a flight from London. His mother had moved to the South of England to be closer to her sister and Jamie planned to spend a night with her *en route* to Scotland.

So she was surprised and secretly delighted on a Sunday evening to answer the door and find Jamie there. He looked lean and fit and she felt her heart turn over.

'Hi,' he said, grinning down at her.

He had caught the sun in the last few weeks and his teeth flashed white against the light tan on his face. Sarah could feel the energy and vitality emanating from him. It was as if his time in Africa had recharged him.

'I hope you don't mind, I just wanted to look in on Calum before I went home. I know he's probably asleep, but just a few minutes?'

Sarah stood back from the door to let him come in. Her legs felt shaky at the sight of him. How she had missed him. She hadn't realised how much until she'd seen him standing before her.

They stole into the nursery. Jamie looked down at his sleeping son and bent slightly to touch his cheek with a gentle finger.

'He's grown since I've been away,' he said, regret tinging his voice. 'SJ, I really don't want to miss another minute of his life. I've missed too much already.' He turned towards Sarah, a wicked glint in his eyes. 'And I missed you, too. Did you miss me? Even a little?'

'We missed you at work. The new consultant is excellent but…' Jamie cocked an eyebrow, encouraging a reluctant Sarah to finish. 'But he's not you,' she admitted finally. 'I kind of got used to working with you again.'

'You only missed me at work?' Jamie raised a disbelieving eyebrow. 'Are you sure? Well, I'm back for a week and I plan spend as much time with Calum as I can. Would it be all right if I came over in the evenings to see him before bedtime? And perhaps we could have some time as a family next weekend? We can take Calum to the zoo or wherever kids like to go when they're his age?'

Sarah couldn't help the pang of disappointment she felt at his words. It was good, of course it was, that he wanted to spend time with her *and* Calum, but if she was honest she'd thought he'd be keen to spend time with her alone.

When he saw Sarah's crestfallen expression

Jamie felt a flicker of triumph. She wasn't as good at hiding her feelings as she'd thought. But he wasn't going to play games with her. He knew he had to be straight with her if she was ever going to trust him.

'Perhaps we could get a babysitter at the weekend? So you and I can have some grown-up time together?' Noting her small smile, he added, 'But not too grown-up, eh?'

Sarah blushed. Damn him! How was he able to read her mind so easily?

'How do you fancy a climb? It'll be like old times. I'm sure Jean won't mind looking after Calum for the day.' Sarah couldn't help the treacherous leap her heart gave at the thought of spending the day with Jamie. They needed to remain friends, she told herself. After all, he was the father of her child and it was important that they got on, even if they didn't live together. However, she suspected she was kidding herself.

True to his word, Jamie came around every evening and most of the days to spend time with Calum. He also arranged for he and Sarah to spend the next Saturday climbing one of the

Munros outside Fort William. The day dawned cool but crisp. The sun shone weakly. It was perfect weather for their climb.

Sarah had rescued her box of climbing gear from the attic the night before, brushing dust off her boots, which hadn't been worn since she and Jamie had last climbed together.

Getting ready that morning, she shook the creases out of her red down-filled jacket and packed the rest of her gear into a small back pack, along with a Thermos of coffee and emergency provisions. When Jamie arrived to collect her, looking ruggedly handsome in his navy mountaineer gear, he insisted on rechecking her harness and ropes.

Satisfied that they had everything necessary, Jamie stood up. 'I don't anticipate that we'll be needing all this gear, but rather safe than sorry,' he said, turning his scrutiny to Sarah. Gently he tucked her fringe under her thermal hat and nodded his approval.

Ignoring the frisson of desire she felt at his touch, she said warningly, 'Jamie—you're doing it again!'

Raising an eyebrow and smiling broadly, Jamie asked with feigned innocence, 'Doing what again, SJ?'

'You know damn well. Treating me like a child. Don't you have any faith in my ability to prepare adequately?'

Jamie held up his hands in mock submission, before turning serious. 'Sorry. But I can't help it—you know how precious you are to me.'

Suppressing the warmth his words gave her, Sarah said briskly. 'Right, let's get going.'

'The weather is forecast to break later today, 'Jamie cautioned as they drove. 'So I want to be off the hill well before it gets dark. We're turning back early this afternoon, whether we've made the summit or not.'

'Fine by me,' Sarah acquiesced. 'I've no plans to spend the night freezing on a mountain.'

Although they chatted comfortably on the way up to Glencoe, there was a sexual tension between them that was palpable. Sarah sneaked glances at Jamie's profile, all too aware of his nearness in the small space of the sports car. When his hand brushed against her leg as he changed gear, Sarah felt charges of electricity course through her body. It was almost a relief to her when they made good time and arrived at the base of the mountain before ten o'clock.

When they got to the top, they ate a picnic of pitta bread sandwiches and hot coffee that Sarah had brought. Jamie found a flat stone near the cairn that marked the summit for them to sit on. The air was a lot colder at the unprotected top, and already clouds were beginning to scud across the sky. Sarah snuggled deeper into her jacket.

Jamie, noticing her shiver, sat behind her and stretched his long legs on either side of hers. He wrapped strong arms around her frame and pulled her close into the embrace of his body. For a moment she resisted before she let herself sink against him, her body absorbing the heat that radiated from him. She felt safe and protected in his arms. She felt his lips brush the top of her head like a whisper.

'I missed you,' Jamie said, his voice deep with emotion. 'Are you sure you didn't miss me? Even the teeniest bit?' he teased.

'I missed you at work.' Sarah repeated the words she had used before. She wasn't ready yet to trust him. Not while there was the slightest chance he was using her to get to Calum.

'Just at work?' Jamie mocked her. 'I see I'll have to do a little bit better.' Gently he turned her face towards him before bringing his lips down hard on hers. She shifted her body to kiss him back. All the weeks and months of missing him were in the kiss. When they eventually broke apart, they were both breathing heavily.

'If it weren't so cold up here, I would—'

'Just as well,' Sarah said primly, a small smile belying her words.

'Let's get you home, then,' Jamie said, his voice heavy with meaning. 'But first I have something to ask you.' He pulled her gently to her feet. He tipped her chin with a long finger so that she was forced to look into his eyes. 'Sarah Jane Carruthers, will you do me the honour of becoming my wife?'

Sarah looked at him, her eyes luminous with unshed tears. Was she about to make the biggest mistake of her life? She thought she probably was, but was powerless to prevent herself. It was as if there were a little demon inside her head, shouting, *Don't do it. You know he's just the same as all men. Remember your father. He told you he loved you, that he'd always be there for you. And he never was—no matter how many times you believed him.* 'I'm sorry, Jamie. I can't say yes. Not yet.'

He let his hands fall to her shoulders. He shook her gently. 'What is it, SJ? Do you need more time?'

She bowed her head in her misery. 'When you left that first time I felt as if something inside me had broken. Something that could never be fixed. The terrible aching loss I felt reminded me of all the times that my father had left me, prom-ising to return. And, of course, he never did—even though he promised. So I built up a shield to protect the child that I was. And when you left, I found that I needed that shield again.'

Jamie listened intently.

'And then when I found out I was pregnant, at first I was terrified.' She raised bleak eyes to his. 'How would I cope? Would I be enough for my child? Didn't every child deserve two loving parents?'

Jamie cursed savagely under his breath and she knew she had hit a nerve. He pulled her into his arms and she let her head rest against his chest.

'Go on,' he encouraged gently.

'Then when I thought there might be something wrong with the baby… I had a raised Down's risk when I was sixteen weeks pregnant, you know?'

'I didn't. At least, not until I overheard you telling the lady with the Down's syndrome child. My God, SJ, I wish I had been there for you.' Jamie's voice was deep with regret.

'It was so hard.' The words began to spill out from Sarah as she remembered the loneliness of having to make those decisions on her own. Of course, her mother had been there and had been a tremendous support, but it hadn't been the same as having the father of her child there beside her. 'I knew that whatever might be wrong, whatever the future might bring, I wanted my child. And at least there would be a part of you that would always belong to me, that no one could take away from me. So I made up my mind to continue the pregnancy. But I also decided that I would never love another man. That from then on, my child would be my life and, apart from my work, my world. We wouldn't rely on anyone else. I had all I needed.'

'I'll never forgive myself for leaving you. I was stupid, selfish, I can see that now, but can't we put the past behind us and start again? I promise you that I will never let you or Calum down again.' His voice was raw with his need to convince her.

Sarah shook her head. 'I don't think so. I wish I could say differently, but I can't. It wouldn't be fair to pretend otherwise.'

He shook her again. 'Won't you at least take a chance? Give me the chance to prove that I love you, that I want you with me? And not just because I want my son?'

'I can't. I'm sorry.' Her voice trembled with the pain. Pain she knew she was inflicting on both of them. But somehow the thought of more pain in the future was worse.

'Damn it, Sarah. I'm only human. Nothing in this life is certain. You and I both know that. Where is the Sarah I used to know? The woman who took risks? Who loved life enough never to hide from it?'

'I don't know. I think she disappeared when you left her that first time.'

'Then I'm sorry, SJ. You're not the woman I thought you were. I can't keep pursuing you if you are never going to change your mind. I'll be back as soon as I can to be with Calum and obviously we'll have to stay in contact as his parents, but apart from that…' He let the words hang in the air. Sarah knew she couldn't blame him. If she couldn't give him what he wanted then she had to set him free to get on with his own life. She supposed she owed him that at least.

'I won't stop you from seeing Calum,' she said through lips that were numb from the effort of holding back the tears.

'I won't let you,' he said. 'I can't make you be with me, but neither can you prevent me from being with my child. Or him being with me.' His voice was flat. Sarah knew she had hurt him, but she also knew that he was angry and confused. Soft flakes of snow began to fall and the sun disappeared behind a cloud. The snow seemed to muffle the outside world until it felt as if nothing else existed except the two of them. The light began to leak from the sky.

'We'd better get back down,' Jamie said.

It was still snowing gently when they reached the bottom of the hill. They had been silent on their journey down, each preoccupied with their own thoughts. There were several other climbers in the car park who had come down from other hills. They exchanged comments about the weather with them as they changed out of their boots in preparation for the journey home.

The snow began to fall in earnest as they drove along the steep and winding road that passed through Glencoe. The snow and clouds made visibility poor and Jamie concentrated on his driving. Sarah knew there was nothing left to say.

Suddenly and without warning the car in front of them skidded on one of the sharp bends. It bounced into the crash barrier before hitting the car in front of it, sending the vehicle straight towards the steep drop at the side of the road.

As Jamie brought his car to a controlled stop, the car that had been hit slammed into the damaged bit of the crash barrier. Sarah and Jamie held their breaths as they hoped the barrier would hold the car. They could make out the shapes of the two passengers—the driver, a young man whose face was stretched in horror, and a child, strapped into a car seat in the back. Jamie pulled his car to the side of the road just as, with a sickening screech of metal, the car tore through the barrier and slid over the side of the road, disappearing from view.

Jamie and Sarah were out of the car almost before it had come to a complete stop.

The car that had caused the accident also pulled over and two young men jumped out, the driver clearly in shock.

'I couldn't stop from hitting them,' he kept repeating. 'Can you see the car? Are they all right?'

'Here,' said Jamie, opening his car boot and removing a couple of triangular warning signs.

He shoved them into the hands of the driver. 'Take these and put them a little way up the road to warn oncoming cars that there's been an accident.' He turned to the passenger. 'Phone for an ambulance and the fire brigade.' And then, as the men stood rooted the spot, he ordered, 'Move it!'

His tone was enough to galvanise them into action. Sarah and Jamie ran to the side of the road. Sarah felt dread close her throat as she peered over the edge. She thought it was unlikely that anyone could have survived the drop. But as they looked, they could see that by some miracle the car had been stopped by an overhang about a third of the way down the slope. In the fading light they could just make out the faint line of a body lying a few metres away from the wrecked vehicle.

'It looks like the driver has been thrown out. That means the child is still in the car,' Sarah told Jamie.

'We need to get down to them,' Jamie said tersely.

'It's too dangerous,' Sarah protested. The

slope was too steep to scramble down. The only way the occupants of the car could be reached was by someone climbing up towards them from the bottom. But that would take time. 'The rescue services should be here shortly.'

But Jamie was already emptying his car boot of the climbing ropes he had brought with him. 'I'm going down.' He said. 'We don't know how long the emergency services will take. I need to assess their injuries. We don't know how badly they are hurt. If we wait, it could be too late.'

As Jamie spoke, one of the men called out. 'There's smoke coming from the car!'

Sarah felt fear close her throat. If the car was on fire, it could explode.

'I'm coming with you,' she said, already beginning to slip on her harness.

'No, you're not! It's too dangerous. The car could go at any time.'

'For the last time, Jamie Campbell, stop telling me what to do.' But Sarah smiled wanly to take the sting out of her words.

Jamie gripped her by the shoulders. 'Good God, woman, think of Calum. He needs his mother.' For a moment a look of anguish crossed his face. 'And I need his mother.' For a moment he brushed her ear with his lips. 'I love you, SJ. I couldn't bear it if anything happened to you.' Jamie looked at her steadily for a long moment. Then, reading the determination in her expression, he made a decision.

'You always were the most stubborn woman. OK, we don't have time to argue. You head for the driver and I'll head for the car. Here, let me check your gear.'

Despite everything, Sarah felt her heart soar. There was no mistaking the expression in those eyes. He did love her. Of course he did. She knew it now—there was no more doubt in her mind!

Sarah tried to open her mouth to tell him that she loved him, too. So very, very much. But as she tried to form the words, Jamie began issuing instructions to her, pointing out the best route for her to take to get to the injured man.

Sarah slipped over the side as Jamie held the rope for her. Within a minute or two she was beside the driver of the car. The man was conscious, though clearly in a lot of pain.

'My daughter. Is she all right?'

'How many of you were in the car?' Sarah asked, dimly aware of Jamie passing her on the way to the car.

'Just me and Ruth. My three-year-old. Where is she? I couldn't control the car.' The man started to moan with pain and fear.

'Jamie—just one other occupant in the car. A little girl.' Sarah called out. Jamie acknowledged her with a lift of his hand. Sarah could see that the smoke from the car was getting thicker. Red flames licked at the car bonnet. The sound of a child's terror and rage filled the air.

'Everything is going to be just fine,' Sarah soothed, checking her patient. Apart from a fractured femur and a few cuts and bruises, he appeared remarkably unharmed. Trying to ignore the burning wreck below her, she strapped his legs together and made him as comfortable as possible. All she could do now was wait for the emergency services to remove the man safely.

She glanced up to see the anxious faces of the bystanders looking towards the car.

Jamie was half in and half out of the back door. The flames were getting bigger by the minute. What on earth was taking him so long? He seemed to be struggling to remove something from the back seat. Was the child pinned in the seat? Sarah felt her blood run cold. Surely there was only a minute or two before it exploded. She knew with a dread that froze her blood that Jamie would never leave the child.

If anything happened to Jamie, she couldn't bear it. How could she have been so stupid? Why had she wasted so much time? Time that they could have been together. Whatever the future brought, she needed to be with Jamie. She, Jamie and Calum together. That was her life, her future, her destiny. She knew now with absolute certainty that Jamie loved her, and not just because she was the mother of his child. He had been prepared to give up everything for her and Calum—to be a permanent part of their lives. He had put his own needs and dreams to one side. And still she hadn't trusted him. What if she lost him now? Before she told him how she felt about him? She closed her eyes and took a couple of deep breaths. She couldn't let herself think like that. She needed to concentrate. Work out how to help him.

He was still struggling to pull the child from the wreckage. Sarah knew she had to go to him. She couldn't stand by and do nothing.

'I'll be back as soon as I can,' she told the driver. 'Just a little longer and we'll have you out of here.'

It only took a few seconds until she was almost down by the car. She could hear the crackle of flames and smell the acrid smoke. In the distance she could hear the sounds of sirens.

Jamie must have sensed her approach. 'Sarah, get out of here!'

'What's wrong? What's taking so long? Why aren't you getting the hell out of there?' she yelled.

'The seat belt's jammed. I can't get the child or its seat out of the car. Don't come any closer.'

Sarah ignored him and slithered the few inches towards him. 'Here.' She handed him her climbing knife. 'Try this.'

'Thanks!' Jamie said 'Now, get going.'

Reluctantly Sarah moved to a safe distance. There was nothing more she could do. She sent a prayer heavenwards.

She heard Jamie's yell of triumph as the girl came loose. Cocooning the child in his arms, he turned away from the car and edged along sideways. As Sarah watched him make his painstakingly slow way, there was a sudden whoosh and the car exploded, rocking the surroundings with the blast. Sarah's heart stopped as she cried out his name.

'Jamie!'

As the smoke cleared she could make out the still form of Jamie lying on the ground. There was no sign of the child. Tears running down her cheeks, Sarah scrambled her way back down the slope, loose gravel causing sharp spasms of pain through her trousers like the sharp bites of tiny predators. She was barely aware of voices calling to her, telling her to stay where she was. She ignored them. She had to get to Jamie. He needed her. One of the rescue team arrived just as she got to Jamie, whose still body showed no sign of life. He had sheltered the child from the worst of the blast with his body. Judging by her loud wails, she seemed to be in one piece.

She shook him roughly. 'Jamie, wake up. Please—I need you. For God's sake don't leave me—I love you.'

Jamie came to slowly. The noise of the blast still rang in his ears. He couldn't hear anything else. Dimly aware of being shaken, he struggled to open his eyes. He saw Sarah bending over him. She was shouting at him. *Typical* he thought. *I'm half-dead and she's still finding something to complain about.*

He looked at her. He saw her lips moving. Tears were cascading down her face. Could he be hearing things? Had the blast addled his brains on top of everything else, or was she really telling him she loved him, would never leave him?

Twenty long minutes later Jamie was being stretchered into the ambulance along with the driver and his daughter. The ambulance would be taking them to the local hospital, from where Jamie would be airlifted to Glasgow if necessary.

He opened his eyes as the paramedics were securing his stretcher.

'Is the child all right?' he asked Sarah.

'She's fine. Frightened but fine. How are you?'

'I'll live.' He smiled painfully. He reached out a hand to Sarah and clasped hers in a surprisingly strong grip. 'You'll have to marry me now.'

'I suppose I will.' Sarah smiled down at him, her eyes awash with tears. 'I guess it's the only way I can keep you from doing crazy things.'

'At least life will never be boring for us,' Jamie murmured, before he lapsed once more into unconsciousness.

Sarah stood at the side of the ship, holding Calum's hand. A few more hours and they'd be docking in Cape Town. From there they would be taking a flight to Johannesburg, before completing the rest of their journey by car. Although she felt a little apprehensive when she thought about the future, she knew with absolute certainty she had made the right decision. The hospital had been sympathetic to her request to take an eighteen-month sabbatical. Especially when she'd been able to convince them that the husband-and-wife team would be perfect locums for the time that she and Jamie would be away. Just thinking of Jamie brought a smile to her lips. While he had recovered in hospital, they had talked for hours, discussing their hopes and dreams. She had realised that Jamie needed to be back in Africa, that he still had work to do there, and had decided that she and Calum would go with him. Her job would be kept open for her.

She felt warm arms enfold her.

'No regrets?' Jamie asked, nibbling her ear.

'None. There's plenty of time for me to be a consultant. This way I can spend more time with Calum. And anyway…' she laughed '…how could I possibly not go to Africa? I have to see this place you love so much for myself.'

'And you're sure you don't mind Sibongele living with us?'

'How could I? I know that Calum and I are always going to have to share you. But somehow I think there is enough love in this family to have some to spare.'

Jamie bent down and scooped his son into his arms before he made his escape. He had just started to toddle in the months leading up to their departure and was constantly trying out his new-found freedom.

'They'll be no more running away, Calum,' Jamie said with mock severity. He looked at Sarah, locking her eyes with his. 'For any of us. Ever again.'

MEDICAL™

Large Print

Titles for the next six months…

May

THE MAGIC OF CHRISTMAS	Sarah Morgan
THEIR LOST-AND-FOUND FAMILY	Marion Lennox
CHRISTMAS BRIDE-TO-BE	Alison Roberts
HIS CHRISTMAS PROPOSAL	Lucy Clark
BABY: FOUND AT CHRISTMAS	Laura Iding
THE DOCTOR'S PREGNANCY BOMBSHELL	Janice Lynn

June

CHRISTMAS EVE BABY	Caroline Anderson
LONG-LOST SON: BRAND-NEW FAMILY	Lilian Darcy
THEIR LITTLE CHRISTMAS MIRACLE	Jennifer Taylor
TWINS FOR A CHRISTMAS BRIDE	Josie Metcalfe
THE DOCTOR'S VERY SPECIAL CHRISTMAS	Kate Hardy
A PREGNANT NURSE'S CHRISTMAS WISH	Meredith Webber

July

THE ITALIAN'S NEW-YEAR MARRIAGE WISH	Sarah Morgan
THE DOCTOR'S LONGED-FOR FAMILY	Joanna Neil
THEIR SPECIAL-CARE BABY	Fiona McArthur
THEIR MIRACLE CHILD	Gill Sanderson
SINGLE DAD, NURSE BRIDE	Lynne Marshall
A FAMILY FOR THE CHILDREN'S DOCTOR	Dianne Drake

MILLS & BOON®

Pure reading pleasure

0408 LP 2P P1 Medical

MEDICAL™

Large Print

August

THE DOCTOR'S BRIDE BY SUNRISE	Josie Metcalfe
FOUND: A FATHER FOR HER CHILD	Amy Andrews
A SINGLE DAD AT HEATHERMERE	Abigail Gordon
HER VERY SPECIAL BABY	Lucy Clark
THE HEART SURGEON'S SECRET SON	Janice Lynn
THE SHEIKH SURGEON'S PROPOSAL	Olivia Gates

September

THE SURGEON'S FATHERHOOD SURPRISE	Jennifer Taylor
THE ITALIAN SURGEON CLAIMS HIS BRIDE	Alison Roberts
DESERT DOCTOR, SECRET SHEIKH	Meredith Webber
A WEDDING IN WARRAGURRA	Fiona Lowe
THE FIREFIGHTER AND THE SINGLE MUM	Laura Iding
THE NURSE'S LITTLE MIRACLE	Molly Evans

October

THE DOCTOR'S ROYAL LOVE-CHILD	Kate Hardy
HIS ISLAND BRIDE	Marion Lennox
A CONSULTANT BEYOND COMPARE	Joanna Neil
THE SURGEON BOSS'S BRIDE	Melanie Milburne
A WIFE WORTH WAITING FOR	Maggie Kingsley
DESERT PRINCE, EXPECTANT MOTHER	Olivia Gates

MILLS & BOON®
Pure reading pleasure

0408 LP 2P P2 Medic